CRITICAL
MASS

BOOK 2 OF THE ATLANTIS LEGACY SERIES

LARRY HAMILTON

Published by Hamilton House Books

www.HamiltonHouseBooks.com

Printed in the United States of America
ISBN: 979-8-9861176-1-4

CHAPTER 1

Cayce Point
North Bimini Island, Bahamas
Present Day

A GUNSHOT SHATTERED THAT perfect day in paradise. Then a second.

Time froze for Matt Flannery. Echoes of the shots rang in his ears, altering his sense of reality. Events revealed themselves in slow motion.

Matt turned his eyes in the direction of the first gunshot. Lucien was falling forward … floating down, down, down. A bright red blossom was growing on the back of his head. Lucien did not attempt to catch himself or break his fall. He was already dead. His eyes were wide and knowing. The gunman had decided to make a point. To let everyone know he was serious. No one saw it coming. Least of all, Lucien.

Matt averted his eyes and gazed toward the second gunman who was now falling slowly forward as in a dream. The back portion of the gunman's skull was missing, and he was slumping down onto the sand near Lucien. Down, down, down. His blood mixing with Lucien's, creating grisly rivulets in the sand. Life forces ebbing and flowing away forever.

Matt now realized where Ghost was. He had concealed himself in a treetop where the forest and beach converged. Ghost had dispatched the fallen gunman with a single shot to the back of the head.

Still feeling as if he was viewing everything on time delay, Matt's eyes were drawn to another movement close by. He observed Jake drawing his combat knife from its holster. Lucien's executioner had been distracted by Ghost's kill shot to the head of his partner and was starting to turn toward Ghost's position to assess the threat. A fatal mistake. The last mistake he would ever make in this life.

Jake took full advantage of the gunman's temporary loss of focus on the hostages—flinging his knife into the assassin's throat in a single fluid motion. Jake followed the knife forward, charging into the surprised man and knocking loose his weapon before he could blink.

Jake had blood in his eyes and fire in his gut. He did not take kindly to losing a comrade, even one as flaky as Lucien. Jake seized the protruding knife handle, forcing it deeper into the gunman's neck while the man flailed against him in a vain attempt to save himself. It ended quickly. Jake twisted the blade and raked it across the man's throat, severing his windpipe and jugulars. The gunman collapsed, authoring his final moments with red sprays and splotches painting the contrasting white sugar sand with unspoken words, writhing and gurgling as he fought desperately against the approaching angel of death. Jake stood defiantly over him, breathing anger and violence from the very depths of his being. His face was contorted into a grim determination. The death angel is always on time, and today had been the appointed time for all three of the dead and dying men on the beach.

Matt was now returning to real-time, surveying the scene that lay around him. Three lifeless bodies on the beach in differing poses. All shared a frozen look of disbelief on their faces. None of the three had expected to die on a cloudless day in this beautiful place. The snowy sand around them was mottled and stained with slowly moving currents of blood. Small, crimson tributaries joined together, creating larger ones, flowing away from the fallen men.

Ghost joined them on the beach, and there was silence except for the breeze in the palms and the sound of waves breaking onshore.

The three surviving men flinched as Kelli pierced the stillness with a sudden, mournful wail and fell to her knees beside Lucien's still body. Lucien was face down, a blood-red halo spreading around his head. Kelli tugged and pulled, trying to turn him over onto his back.

His limp body begrudgingly yielded to her efforts, and she started squeezing Lucien's left hand between the two of hers. She sobbed and heaved, laboring to breathe. Matt moved to her side, knelt, and placed his hand on Kelli's back. He didn't know what to do. What can anyone do at a moment like this? He was numb. Jake and Ghost stood awkwardly beside them. They didn't know what to say or do, either. Battle-hardened or not, this was a difficult moment for all of them.

Jake felt guilty for failing to protect Lucien. He should have been more vigilant that night at Big John's Bar, where Lucien was kidnapped. Experience should have warned him not to let anyone leave the group alone, not even to the restroom. He had been negligent. Had let his guard down. He knew better.

Ghost was inwardly second-guessing his strategy of letting the scene play out before he opened fire. The last thing he had expected was for the gunman to execute Lucien at the moment he did. But he knew always to expect the unexpected and to be one step ahead of the game. He should have neutralized the threat sooner. He had been late to react. He knew better.

Matt was rethinking his actions of the day as well.

Would it have made a difference if he had handed over the relics as Lucien had requested? Would Lucien still be alive? Would any of them still be alive? Would that have bought more time for Jake and Ghost to intercede? Would it have been enough?

His questions would forever go unanswered.

Kelli looked up through her overflowing, swollen eyes at the three men gathered around her near Lucien's quiet form. Tears soaked her face, streaming down her cheeks, leaving dark, damp splotches on her shirt. Kelli felt and experienced things on a very deep level. If anyone had asked them at that moment, the three men beside her would have agreed she was a better person than any of them.

She spoke haltingly between breathless sobs as her voice quivered uncontrollably.

"We didn't … even … get … a chance … to … say goodbye … to … Lucien. He was gone. Just … just like that! Those … those … rotten bastards … they didn't … have … to … kill him!"

Jake cleared his throat and tried to speak in a low, comforting tone.

"Kelli, they were going to kill all of us. They just got Lucien first. If Ghost hadn't been hiding in that tree, we'd all be dead right now."

"I know … damn it! I … know. But … it's … so … so … sad. For him to die this way … I … I … just can't … believe it. He was … one of us. He was … one of us."

CHAPTER 2

Cayce Point
North Bimini Island, Bahamas

THE SHOCK WAS SLOWLY receding, and Matt's brain was struggling desperately to clear. He knew they needed to make critical decisions and make them quickly. He stood up from where he had knelt to comfort Kelli and broke the solemn silence, smothering and uncomfortable, that hovered over them.

Matt looked around at Jake and Ghost and spoke in a low but serious tone. "We need to decide where to go from here, guys. This is a hell of a situation we're in, and I don't know any good way out of it. Jake, you've got a lot more experience at this sort of thing than I do. Any ideas?"

Jake had already been pondering their options. It was a complicated scenario.

"Well, Matt, it depends on how you want to play it. We can dispose of the bodies and cut and run. Try to get back to the mainland before any more of these crazies show up. But, I'm pretty sure you won't choose that option."

"No, I can't do that. I don't give a damn about those two murdering assholes over there, but I can't just leave Lucien here. He deserves a decent burial. I think we owe him that."

Kelli had sat up and was watching them intently, waiting to see if they would do the right thing.

"Okay, I'm good with that. I already figured that wouldn't fly. The next option would be to contact the local authorities and try to come up with a story that won't land our asses in jail."

They thought on that for a moment. Matt said what everyone was thinking.

"I don't think we could ever concoct a story good enough to get us out of this mess easily or quickly … or at all. They'll hold us for God knows how long. We can't prove who started what. They could decide we're the bad guys. Hell, we rolled into their quiet little town with a shot-up boat, and now this? And, they'll confiscate all our belongings, including the artifacts. They'll claim we stole a national treasure, and that alone would land us in prison. We can't allow that to happen. Lucien will have died in vain, and our grandfathers will turn over in their graves."

Jake paused a bit.

"You are right on all counts, Pardner. I'm glad you understand that. There *is* a third option. It'll be tricky, but it's all I have right now. I can call in a favor from my contacts at the CIA. I could reach them from your sat phone and arrange to get us out of here in one piece."

Matt stared at Jake while the wheels in his head turned furiously, searching for another option. He looked at Ghost, who was nodding in quiet agreement with Jake.

"Isn't there some other way, Jake? They'll want more than a thank you if they come get us."

"Yes and no. First of all, if my people know that me and Ghost are in harm's way, they'll pick us up, no questions asked. That's the unwritten code we live by. I can also request the use of a safe house if you want. And yes, there will be questions at some point. But we'll be safe for the time being, and it will give you time to decide how you're going to handle all this."

"What about the bodies?"

"We can deep-six the two pieces of shit over there, and I'll make arrangements for Lucien's body to be taken back home."

"You can do that?"

Jake smiled a bit and looked at Ghost, who was smiling, too.

"I wouldn't offer it if I couldn't do it. You've trusted me this far Compadre. You'll just have to trust me a little longer … *maybe a lot longer.*"

CHAPTER 3

Brown's Marina
North Bimini Island, Bahamas

THE FOUR SURVIVORS OF the ambush at Cayce Point dragged the bodies of the two dead gunmen into the water. Matt and Kelli waded back to the beach and busied themselves with preparations for leaving on the rental boat. They did not have much stomach for what they knew would happen next.

Jake and Ghost performed the same procedures on the two dead gunmen that they had carried out on the lifeless bodies of the assault teams at Key Biscayne. They used their knives to open strategically placed gashes in the corpses that would allow body gases to escape as the bodies decomposed. This guaranteed they would not become floaters, which might attract unwanted attention. After completing their gruesome surgeries, Jake and Ghost walked the bodies out as far as they could, then swam out further, pulling the bodies behind them. Once satisfied the water was of sufficient depth, they released the bodies to settle into watery graves. It was almost a certainty sharks or other predator fish would be attracted to the bloody corpses and dispose of them in short order.

They considered sinking the boat the gunmen had arrived in, but the water was too shallow. It was decided the best course of action would be to pull the anchor on the second boat and let it float away from the beach where the confrontation had occurred. The currents and winds would decide where it should go. It would just be a mystery to whoever found it.

Matt rummaged through all the storage lockers and cubbyholes on their rental boat and discovered an old blue tarp. They solemnly wrapped their departed friend in it and laid him on the floor of the boat. The unpleasant chores were now complete, and they made a hasty exit from Cayce Point, a mystical place that had presented them with both revelation and horror.

Once back in Brown's Marina, Matt guided the rental boat alongside the stern of the *Nice Catch*. Matt and Kelli boarded the *Catch* while Jake and Ghost gathered the tools and artifacts and handed them up to Matt and Kelli, who stowed them onboard the bigger boat. The last thing they brought aboard the *Catch* was the blue tarp holding the remains of Lucien Bart.

They carefully lifted him up and over the side of the rental boat and onto the stern of the *Catch*. Then they decided to place his body below decks in the cabin he had once occupied. The stateroom was air-conditioned and would maintain the body in an acceptable condition until further transport could be arranged.

Matt checked to make sure they had removed all their belongings from the rental boat, then started the outboards and steered it away from the *Nice Catch*. He hardly took notice of the clear blue sky and seafoam green water surrounding him as he delivered the boat to the rental company. There was no time, and he was not in the right frame of mind for admiring the scenery, no matter how magical. He soon returned to Brown's Marina, hurrying, yet trying not to look conspicuous.

He checked in at the harbormaster's office where he was assured by Johnnie that Lucien had not shown up or left a message. Matt thanked Johnnie and informed him they would be leaving the marina soon, but the *Catch* would be staying until the insurance company decided its fate. He told Johnnie to keep his credit card on file to cover slip fees as long as needed. Matt settled his bill, collected the paid receipts, and shook Johnnie's hand.

Matt winced at the thought of leaving his beloved boat behind, but he had no choice. He had to focus on survival and protecting his friends as well as his discoveries. He would not let Lucien's death be in vain.

He walked the short distance back to the *Catch* and paused on the dock where she rocked gently at berth. He stopped and squinted through the dazzling sunlight at his disfigured boat. The sight of her caused a cold, hard ball to form in the pit of his stomach. He began to chew on his lower left lip, screwing his face into a grimace. Every time he looked at his boat, it felt like a punch in the gut. He would never get used to seeing it in this condition.

The once sleek, proud ship was a mangled wreck. The observation tower and flying bridge were destroyed, much of the structure missing. What few parts remained hung off to one side like a dangling and useless broken arm. The cabin below had sustained serious collateral damage as well. Part of the back wall had been blown off and was now covered with a blue tarp. It looked obscene on this beautiful craft. The salon was in tatters. Burled, polished wood tables splintered and scattered like firewood kindling. White leather lounges gashed, torn, and discolored with burn marks. Only the galley to the front, most of the lower helm, and the staterooms below were still intact.

He stepped off the dock and onto the rear deck of the *Catch*. He retrieved his camera from the owner's cabin that he and Kelli had shared on happier trips and took extensive photos of the damaged boat. He needed to forward the pictures to his insurance company as soon as he got a chance so they could dispatch an adjustor and determine how they would handle the claim. The more he surveyed the wide-ranging damage to his boat, the more he feared it would be declared a total loss. If so, the insurance company would compensate him and sell the boat for salvage. He would have money to replace the boat, but in his heart, he felt it was irreplaceable. He and this boat had a history. It had been a dream fulfilled. They had shared some great times and survived some close calls together. He shook his head trying to make the specter of losing his beloved *Catch* go away as well as attempting to banish the other disturbing images that were haunting his mind. He could not believe all that had happened.

The losses were piling up—his boat, his peaceful life, and now Lucien.

Would this be the end of the killing and destruction? Or, was it just the beginning? How could he protect the artifacts without continuing to put those around him in danger? Or, could he protect the artifacts at all?

Perhaps, it was all just foolish thinking on his part. A pipe dream.

He had no answers to these questions, so he headed to the galley where the others were gathered. He needed to refocus on matters at hand.

CHAPTER 4

Brown's Marina
North Bimini Island, Bahamas

Matt pulled back the blue tarp covering the lounge entrance to the boat and worked his way through the wreckage to the galley where Kelli, Jake, and Ghost were quietly working through a first round of cold beers. Kelli reached into the refrigerator and grabbed one for Matt. They all wore somber looks on their faces that resembled funeral masks. The galley was where Lucien's sense of humor and culinary skills had shone through the brightest. They all felt his presence as if he was still there with them. Perhaps he was. The loss hung over them like a low, sad cloud.

Matt took a long pull off his beer and shared the reverent silence with them for a few moments. But, as hard as it was to focus, circumstances demanded that he move the situation forward. Time was working against them.

"This has been a tough day, and we're all feelin' it right now. Lucien might have been a loose cannon, but he didn't deserve what he got. I know we're all thinking that if we had done something differently, he might still be alive. But we all did the best we knew to do in the situation and moment we were in. We're going to have to be okay with that and not second-guess and beat ourselves up over it. I'm pretty sure that if Lucien was here with us right now, he would want us to drink up in his memory, and remember him for the crazy, fun-loving guy he was. I propose a toast to the memory of our fallen friend and fellow musketeer."

With that, all raised their bottles to the heavens. Matt continued with the toast.

"To Lucien, our friend and partner. May you enter into the pearly gates under full sails and blue skies."

The four of them clinked beer bottles, said "Hear, hear!" in unison, and took long, solemn drinks in honor of Lucien. Matt looked at Kelli as he brought his bottle down and observed the fountains in her beautiful eyes opening again. He glanced around and noticed she was not the only one with moist eyes. The men all began looking away from one another, clearing their throats, wiping eyes with backs of sleeves and bare arms, and began to shuffle around for more beer and maybe a snack.

Matt sniffled, took a deep breath, and addressed Jake. He had to keep pushing the situation forward, no matter how difficult the timing might be.

"Jake, what's this going to look like once you make that call to your buddies at the Shop?"

Jake blinked away some telltale moisture from his eyes and cleared his throat. "Not sure. Depends on what assets they have in the area. Most likely, they'll send a plane or boat to pick us up and take Lucien wherever I designate."

"You think we'll be getting any last-minute visits from our old friends before we can get out of here?"

"I doubt it. We're in a busy spot here at the marina, and since they only sent two men on that last attack, it tells me they may be running out of local operatives at the moment. They might have started with deep resources, but we've made them pay a steep price for coming after us. They've lost a lot of manpower over the last few days."

"Yeah, I was a little surprised that there were only two of them this time. So, do you have any idea where we could go once your guys pick us up?"

"I'll have to ask my handler if we can use a safe house, and if he agrees, he'll pick one for us. It could be anywhere."

Ghost cut into the conversation. "I have a safe house we can use if you want. It's completely off the grid. Not even my handler knows about it to the best of my knowledge. I've been putting it together for years. I'm planning on retiring there soon."

Jake shot him a surprised and amused look. "Ghost, you been holdin' out on me?"

"As you like to say, Jake … need-to-know basis!"

Jake chuckled, and Ghost grinned. The others watched the show from the outside looking in.

"Alright, friend, you got me there. Where's this secret hideout you've been working on?"

"It's back in the hills of eastern Kentucky where I grew up. It's a log house on a ridge where very few people live. And, everybody that lives there knows everybody else. So, a stranger sticks out like a sore thumb."

"How secure is it?" Jake asked.

"About as secure as it can be." Ghost replied. "Unobstructed 360-degree sightlines. Limited egress, one road in and out. Only visible from the air and nothing unusual to see even then. I've got the usual assortment of trip and proximity alarms, safe room, weapons and ammo, satellite communications gear, and a couple of four-wheelers. It's pretty self-sustaining; generator, solar power, well water."

Jake whistled his appreciation for what Ghost had described. "Damn! That's better than the safe houses that Uncle Sam provides!"

"Yeah, I thought you'd like it," Ghost proudly responded.

"Okay, does everyone agree to take Ghost up on his generous offer?" Jake asked.

"Never look a gift horse in the mouth," Matt said.

"I always wanted to spend some time in the hills!" Kelli added.

"Alright, Ghost. Your place it is. How do we get there?" Jake asked.

"We can fly into Blue Grass Airport in Lexington. They're able to accommodate government planes. I'll have one of my relatives drive my Jeep over to the airport and leave it in long-term parking. He knows where the key is and where to leave it."

"Looks like you've thought of everything, Pardner."

"Not everything. What will we do with Lucien?"

"He needs to go home where he can have a funeral with his family present," Kelli said. "Matt, you told me that Ken did a background check on all of us when we were at the Station. He should have information on Lucien's immediate family. Could you call him on the sat phone and find out who to contact?"

"Sure, I can do that," Matt replied.

"No need, Matt," Jake interjected. "My people will have all the info we need to make arrangements. There's not a whole lot they don't know or can't find out. I'll have him flown to a holding facility in the Tampa area where he can be picked up by a funeral director of his family's choosing. There's a big Air Force base there, and that's the area he was from."

"But what are we going to tell his family?" Matt asked. "They'll want to know what happened to him."

"We'll have to create a cover story since we can't tell them the truth," Jake said. "The CIA are experts at misinformation and that sort of thing. They'll do a good job. Probably something along the lines of a fatal late-night robbery by an unknown assailant while Lucien was vacationing in the islands. They can even create false news stories if need be."

Everyone nodded. Sad, but that's the way it would have to be.

Matt picked up the sat phone, stared at it like it was a poisonous snake, chewed on his lip, and handed it to Jake. "Make the call."

CHAPTER 5

On Board the Catch
North Bimini Island, Bahamas

WITHIN AN HOUR OF Jake making the call to his CIA handler, a nondescript fishing trawler pulled alongside the *Nice Catch* and took Lucien's body aboard where it would rest in a refrigerated compartment normally used to preserve the day's haul of fish. The trawler's captain had instructions to transport the body to South Bimini Island, where the main airport was located. The remains would be loaded onto an unmarked cargo plane and flown to MacDill AFB in Tampa, where it would be held until the family could make arrangements to have it picked up and brought home.

The four of them stood and watched as the trawler pulled away in the fading light. They inwardly said goodbye to their friend. They would not be able to attend his funeral for a multitude of reasons. This was the final farewell.

Soon after the trawler cleared the area, a large twin-engine seaplane appeared in the sky and approached the harbor. The unmarked, silver plane splashed, bounced, and wallowed to a landing in the channel near the *Catch*. It taxied to a position near the boat and waited while Matt lowered the dinghy into the water and ferried the four passengers and their personal belongings over to the plane. It was nearing sunset when they settled aboard their new ride. Matt had paid one of the marina attendants a healthy tip to retrieve the dinghy and secure it back on board the *Catch* once they left.

Drawing a lot of curious stares from nearby onlookers, the big plane roared, pitched, and fought its way off the water, lumbering into the air just in time to showcase a breathtaking view of the sun disappearing into the western horizon with the moon making a cameo appearance to the east. Matt looked down at the silhouette of the *Nice Catch*, framed in the golden rays of late-day sunlight with the moon watching over it. He swallowed a lump in his throat and looked away. He felt he was abandoning her.

Goodbye for now, old friend. I hope to see you again soon.

The seaplane noisily ferried them the short distance to the Reserve Air Force Base at Homestead, Florida, where they would transfer to a government jet tasked with taking them to Lexington, Kentucky. Darkness had fallen hard, and the day had been mentally, physically, and emotionally exhausting. It seemed as if this day had begun a week ago. So much had happened in the last twelve hours, that it was difficult for them to fathom it all.

Once they were on the ground, Jake spoke to the base commander at Homestead and arranged secure sleeping quarters for them. They all needed a night of uninterrupted rest before continuing their journey. Once in their private quarters—typical military room with two twin-size beds, chair, and dresser—Matt and Kelli dropped the bags to the floor, scooted the twin beds together, and collapsed onto the mattresses. The bed was relatively small, but they were quite content to spoon up and make it work. Jake and Ghost each had a room nearby.

Matt held Kelli tightly as they fought off the horrendous memories of the day and attempted sleep. The day had held too much. Too, too much. They had watched shocking, realistic images of an entire civilization being destroyed. Only a few minutes later, they had witnessed their friend being murdered right in front of them. More than any day should hold … or anyone should have to bear in one short trip of the sun.

After several tortured minutes of squeezing their eyes shut against the intrusive thoughts and memories, they began to drift. But not before Matt felt a few more quiet sobs softly escaping from Kelli's tortured heart.

Matt forced himself to stay awake until he heard Kelli's mourning subside, replaced by the rhythmic, deep breathing of sound slumber. He now felt free to join her and drift away, praying he wouldn't dream.

Morning came fast. Too fast.

Matt sat up with a start, rousing Kelli out of a deep sleep. The sun was pushing through the curtains of the room, urgently beckoning them forward into another day. They had kicked off their shoes and slept in their clothes, so it did not take long for them to slip back into their shoes, grab their bags, and go out to see if Jake and Ghost were up and about.

The door to Jake's room was open, and he and his belongings were nowhere to be seen. Same with Ghost's room. Matt could smell coffee down the hall, so he followed his nose and headed in that direction with Kelli in tow. They rounded the corner to the mess hall, and there sat Jake and Ghost with full plates of eggs, bacon, and toast on the table in front of them and hot mugs of coffee in their hands.

"Hello, sleepyheads! I was afraid I was going to have to come get you," Jake quipped. "Grab some grub, and let's get this show on the road. The jet's fueling up, and it's about ready to go."

As Matt chewed on a breakfast roll, he thought about the private jet waiting for them. Jake could summon that level of resources from the government with just a phone call?

"Damn, Jake. You must have friends in really high places. A seaplane? A private jet?"

"More like friends in really low places," Jake replied with a smirk. "These 'friends' as you call them, owe me a pretty big stack of favors. I just called in a couple, that's all."

"Where do they get all these planes and boats? They got to us in no time."

"Uncle Sam's in the drug business. Remember the Contra hearings?"

"Yeah, wasn't the CIA selling illegal drugs to fund covert operations so they wouldn't have to go through congressional approval to get the money they wanted?"

"Bingo. They still run drugs, but not as much as they used to. The government funds a huge black ops budget now that's entirely off the books, and there's almost no congressional oversight, so they can get their funding 'legally' for the most part now. As far as having all these boats and planes, when they bust a drug-running syndicate, they confiscate the planes and boats and money for their own use. Over the years, they've built up quite a fleet, and a lot of it is concentrated in the islands near the U. S. mainland. Now, you've got Homeland Security, ATF, DEA, Immigration, Coast Guard, Navy, Air Force, CIA, and God knows who else, all working in the area."

"Have they asked you any questions yet?" Matt asked.

"No, but they will soon enough. Company favors always come with strings attached. But, in the business that Ghost and I were in, you come when called and ask why later. They know me well enough to understand that I don't cry wolf unless there's a wolf."

"Have you decided what you're going to tell them?

"Other than the information about finding the relics, I'll tell them the truth, or at least something with a kernel of truth in it. The best lie always has a certain amount of truth to it. I'll try to sell it as a piracy story. I don't think they'll buy it, but it might slow them down a little while they look for the real story."

Matt took another sip of his coffee and looked at Kelli, then Ghost and Jake. "Thanks for taking care of Lucien."

"No need to thank me. He was a fellow combatant. We don't leave our brothers behind if we can help it. Glad I could get him home."

With that statement, Jake noisily slid back his chair and rose from the table while tipping up and draining his coffee mug.

"Alright, let's swallow this food and get a cup of java to go. Our plane is waiting."

CHAPTER 6

Blue Grass Airport
Lexington, Kentucky

THE GLEAMING WHITE PRIVATE jet, plain and unmarked as was the case with all the planes and boats that Jake had summoned, touched down, skipped once, then rolled smoothly on the runway at Blue Grass Airport.

During the approach, the four passengers could see the meticulously groomed horse farms of the Bluegrass spread out below them as far as the eye could see. It was winter, which dulled the green of the grass, but did not diminish the unique beauty of the region. The grass that grew in horse country took on a blue-green appearance due to the limestone rock that lay under the soil. It was said to impart magical growth and performance properties to the horses that were fortunate enough to grow up and graze in those picturesque pastures.

The long, running lines of black and white wooden rail fences divided paddocks and pastures where playful young colts frolicked under the watchful gaze of their mothers. The grand barns and manor houses recalled images of a bygone era of privileged nobility. For those that owned and occupied these estates, a modern form of aristocracy continued to exist.

To the west, the land stretched flat and featureless, except for the tall buildings of downtown Louisville poking up in the distance. To the east, the foothills of the Appalachians rose to greet them, imposing guardians of the people who lived there. Except for the pines and evergreens, the trees were mostly barren, having dropped their fall leaves and exposing the brown hills on which they stood.

Matt, Kelli, Jake, and Ghost peered out the plane windows as the jet taxied around to a private, secure area of the airport where they would not have to clear customs or answer questions.

They grabbed their bags, deplaned, exited the terminal area through an employee side gate, and walked the short distance to long-term parking where Ghost pointed to his waiting Jeep. Ghost kneeled beside the black Wrangler and reached up into the wheel well near the engine compartment where he located the hidden key. He pressed the button on the key fob to unlock the doors and walked around to the back, where he opened the rear window to allow everyone to deposit their bags in the small cargo area. It was a clear, crisp November morning, so they all donned their jackets and climbed into the Jeep, Ghost in the front driver's seat with Jake riding shotgun, and Kelli and Matt in the back. It was a noticeable temperature change from South Florida where they had been only a couple of hours earlier.

Ghost paid the parking attendant and gunned the Jeep out onto US 60 East, where he took the 421 Bypass around Lexington to Paris Pike and then linked up with I-64 East, which would take them into hill country. An hour and a half from the time they had landed in Lexington, Ghost took the Morehead exit off I-64 and wound through the picturesque little college town. The flat lands of the bluegrass had given way to the foothills of the Appalachians at this point in their journey. Morehead's main street looked like something out of a '50s movie with an assortment of five-and-dime stores, drugstores with lunch counters, and old buildings with dressed up façades. These holdovers from a not-too-distant past now lived alongside the newer buildings occupied by banks and clothing stores. A new Walmart and several chain motels had sprung up near the interstate exit. Morehead State University took up a large portion of the east side of town. Only a couple miles out of town past the university and continuing east, Ghost turned right onto State Route 32 and headed into hill country.

The Wrangler climbed higher and higher into the eastern Kentucky hills, negotiating sharp switchbacks and turns. The man-made scenery thinned out. Only the occasional general store with rusty, antiquated signs hanging off them or mobile homes and simple ranch houses perched on hillsides and ridge tops encroached on the natural setting. Plainly dressed people waved from their front yards or porches as you passed. Some of the men wore overalls and ball caps with logos of tobacco companies or their favorite automakers. Others wore hunting jackets or hoodies. Camo patterns were the common theme on all of it. The older women wore simple house dresses with sweaters and the younger ones, blue jeans, and sweatshirts. It did not matter if they knew you or not, it was a tradition in these parts to raise a friendly hand to all who passed by … and take a look at your license plate. They liked to keep track of who was coming and going in their part of the world. The residents were genuinely friendly, humble, and charitable unless you gave them reason not to be. It was best to stay on their good side and show them simple respect.

Ghost continued driving in a long upward climb until the road leveled out on top of a ridgeline. From this elevated vantage point, they could see other ridges running off in the distance like the arms of a giant starfish. The scenery was remote yet breathtaking.

Great place for a safe house, Jake thought to himself.

After following the main two-lane state road along the top of the ridgeline for a few miles, Ghost slowed the Jeep and turned left onto a well-maintained gravel road that pitched downward into a gulley, across a small wooden bridge, up the other side to the top of another ridgeline, through a thickly forested area, and abruptly ended at a steel gate with a security pad and camera sitting off to the driver's side. The sudden appearance of modern technology seemed strange and out of place in this setting.

As he rolled down his window, Ghost punched in a code that triggered the security gate to retract. After clearing the gate, it slid quickly back into place behind them. The Jeep proceeded another hundred yards or so, turned a sharp corner to the left, and the road suddenly widened into a large clearing, and a log home stood straight ahead. It was situated at the backside of the clearing with the parking area in front of it. It featured a front porch that traversed the full length of the house. Sitting on the porch were four inviting rocking chairs and a wooden swing suspended from chains looped onto eye hooks screwed into the wood of the porch ceiling. The house itself was constructed of maple-colored wood logs that gave it a cozy mountain cabin feel. The roof was dark green sheet metal, and there was a large stone chimney poking up through it. A loft with windows was visible along the roofline as well.

Ghost swung the Jeep in a wide circle, stopping close to the house. He backed up a bit, positioning the rear of the vehicle toward the house for easier unloading and fast getaways, and jumped out. The others followed his lead and started spilling out as well. They walked as a group to the rear of the Jeep to retrieve their bags, and as they opened the rear cargo door, four men appeared from a thicket of nearby trees that ringed the parking area. They were brandishing large caliber rifles with scopes and were dressed in full camo gear.

The gunman closest to them immediately barked an order.

"Don't move a damned muscle."

CHAPTER 7

West Palm Beach, Florida
Dominion Winter Estate

JORDAN DOMINION PACED BACK and forth across the highly polished, imported wood floor of the den in his palatial West Palm Beach winter home. He had every reason to be happy and content. Immense wealth, international fame, vast power and influence, beautiful and devoted wife, and two healthy children. But he was neither happy nor content. He was a ruthless, driven man. Nothing would ever be enough. The world itself would never be adequate to satisfy his boundless ambition. He felt entitled to anything he desired in this life, including those damned Atlantis artifacts.

He was not accustomed to failure, and his operatives had failed him repeatedly. Time to fulfill a promise and install a new game plan with a different team and head coach.

He shut the heavy doors to the study, checked his watch, and sat down in a large, overstuffed wingchair. The perfectly manicured lawn, picturesque gardens, sparkling fountains, and pool located on the backside of his estate could be viewed perfectly from where he sat. Such a peaceful, serene vista lay outside his window. A sharp contrast to the chaotic war-room of his mind. He opened a drawer in the side table next to the chair, pulled out a disposable cell phone, and made a call. Peace and serenity held no appeal for him. Only power … and more power.

It was time to settle an account.

He heard the phone ring twice, and then a voice quickly responded on the other end of the line.

"Yes, Mr. Dominion."

"Are you in position?"

"I am."

"Good. I am now initiating the plan we discussed. I will be placing the call to your predecessor as soon as I end this call with you."

"Understood, Mr. Dominion."

"Very well. Do not fail me. You now see the consequences of failure."

Jordan Dominion terminated the call and calmly pulled another burner phone out of the drawer and punched in a different set of digits. The person on the other end answered after one ring.

"Good morning, Mr. Dominion."

"Good morning to you as well, Mr. Petrov. Am I to understand that you and the Brotherhood failed to secure the relics yet again?"

"Yes, but I can explain it all, sir. You see, they had a—"

"Excuse me, Mr. Petrov, but it seems we have had this same conversation on multiple occasions, and I am always given news of the same failures and excuses and poor outcomes."

"I know, Mr. Dominion, but—"

"Did I not give you more than ample resources to carry out your missions, Mr. Petrov? Everything you told me you needed to be successful?"

"Yes, sir. But there was no way to anticipate—"

"Were you not paid handsomely for your ability to anticipate and overcome obstacles, Mr. Petrov?"

"You were more than generous, sir. That was never a question."

"So … if you were me, Mr. Petrov, what *would* be the question? I provided ample resources and manpower, clear directives, and yet you continually disappointed me. If you remember, I also made a promise to you concerning our business arrangement. Do you recall what that promise was?"

Petrov's voice was starting to tighten and become higher pitched.

"No, sir, I do not remember what promise you are referring to."

"Think a little harder, my dear friend. We discussed accountability and responsibility should you squander all the assets I provided you with. Did we not talk about the penalty for failure?"

"Well, yes sir we did, but—"

"Do you believe that I am a man of my word, Petrov?"

"Of course, Mr. Dominion. Everyone knows you are."

"Well, since I have a reputation for being a man of my word, it would be important for me to uphold that reputation, would it not? Otherwise, no one would take me seriously, and I would be viewed as weak and vulnerable. Nobody wants to be viewed as weak, do they, Mr. Petrov?"

Petrov could see where this was going and knew he was being maneuvered into a corner. *He had to make Dominion understand that none of this was his fault!*

"Of course, I can see why that is important to you, sir. But, please let me explain to you what happened and why I could not have prevented it."

"Okay, Petrov. Fair enough. Explain to me what happened to all those men at Key Biscayne or how we lost our last two Brotherhood operatives at Cayce Point?"

"Well … uh … as I have stated, sir, that was highly irregular and a total mystery. I found no trace of any of those men."

"So, you cannot explain your failure in those situations? Or what happened to my expensive assets?"

Petrov had the sinking feeling he could not successfully extract himself from this predicament and was already planning in his head how he might escape and disappear for a while until he had time to figure out a way to make amends with his employer.

"Not yet, Mr. Dominion. But I assure you that given time, I will get to the bottom of all of it."

Jordan Dominion picked up his other cell phone and placed a call to the person he had spoken with initially. As soon as the other party answered, he hit the off button on the phone, ending the call. The signal was given.

Amir Kabil could see Petrov clearly in the crosshairs of the powerful scope mounted on his rifle. He had now been given the order to proceed with the mission. He took a deep breath, relaxed into his weapon, and focused on the target.

"Ah! So, there it is, Mr. Petrov. You cannot account for my assets or the relics. Do you even know where our targets might be at this point in time?"

"No, sir. I had a local fisherman watching their boat and reporting to me. He said they left by seaplane to an undetermined location."

"I see. You do understand that I have no choice but to fulfill my promise to you, don't you, Mr. Petrov? I am known to be a man of my word."

"Please, Mr. Dominion, if you would just give me a chance to—"

Kabil squeezed the trigger on the powerful rifle, and Petrov's head exploded in mid-sentence. Petrov had been standing on a deserted beach south of Miami as he talked with Jordan Dominion. Kabil had been commissioned by Dominion to carry out the pledge he had made to Petrov. This was Amir's first step in earning the trust of Dominion and using him to create worldwide jihad.

Kabil's phone rang. It was Dominion.

"Have you completed your mission, Mr. Kabil?"

"Yes, Mr. Dominion. Target is eliminated."

"Excellent. I will expect pictures from you shortly confirming the status of Mr. Petrov. You now understand the price for failure, do you not?"

"You have made it very clear, sir. I will not fail."

"Let us hope not. It's time to proceed with the next part of your mission, Mr. Kabil. Do you have your men briefed and ready?"

"I do."

"Then, move swiftly. Time is becoming an issue."

CHAPTER 8

Safe House
Johnson's Ridge, Kentucky

Matt, Kelli, and Jake had frozen in place and were looking at the gunmen with facial expressions of shock and disbelief.

Matt's head was spinning. *How could this be? How could anyone know where we are and be this far ahead of us?*

Suddenly, Ghost let out a whoop and ran straight toward the gunman who had commanded them not to move, leaving his fellow travelers stunned. Ghost embraced the man who had threatened them, and the other three gunmen joined in a big group hug with Ghost. The other three new arrivals stood slack-jawed and confused at the rear of the Jeep.

Ghost was wearing a big grin on his face as he turned to his friends. "Sorry about that. My relatives have a warped sense of humor at times, as you've just seen. Let me introduce you. The one here that decided this would be funny is my first cousin and brother by a different mother, Perry. He's a little crazy, but mostly in a good way. The other three are my cousins, Dale, Wayne, and Eddie."

Perry Johnson, tall and lanky, stepped forward wearing an easy grin and extended his hand to all three visitors. "Welcome to Johnson Ridge, folks."

CHAPTER 9

Cocoa Beach, Florida

CAROL FLANNERY BROWSED IN a casual women's wear shop near Cocoa Beach, looking for a new running suit to add to her wardrobe for the upcoming winter season. The cooler weather would soon blow in, and she wanted to look her best when it did. But she was having difficulty focusing on the racks of clothing around her. Troubling things were going on in her family, and she wasn't sure how to resolve it. She believed it was her job as the chief negotiator and peacemaker among them, to smooth over and repair family issues, a responsibility she took very seriously. It had been her life's work for the most part. Her brow furrowed, and she chewed on her lower lip as she absentmindedly moved things around on the rack in front of her.

Carol was a trim, attractive woman who was determined to defy her age of fifty-eight years. She worked out regularly and ate healthy other than her daily glass or two of Chardonnay. She was medium height and build with reddish-brown hair and the same gray-blue eyes that her son Matt had inherited. She had passed on her habit of lower lip chewing to him as well. She had paid to have a couple of vanity procedures done, but only minor ones. She had passed up a promising career in healthcare administration to devote herself to raising her two children, Cindy and Matthew. She chose to take care of everything at home, so her husband, Joseph, could pursue his career with NASA. She occasionally experienced a tinge of regret over what she might have accomplished professionally, especially now that the kids were grown and living busy lives of\ their own. But for the most part, she was content with her choices. Life was all about choices. Joseph was always gracious about crediting her with his success at climbing the corporate and political ladder at NASA, and that made her choices easier to accept.

Their family life had always been great for the most part, but as with all families, there had been bumps in the road. The most persistent and painful problem was this estrangement between Matt and his father. There had never been enough of Joseph to go around during his ascent through the NASA hierarchy. Carol understood and accepted the situation, Cindy adjusted, but Matt struggled with it. He had gravitated to Joseph's father instead. Bill Flannery had been a healthy and stimulating influence on Matt, but he was not able to replace what should have been there between Matt and his father. The distance between Matt and his dad had grown over the years, quietly boiling beneath the surface of Matt's emotions like molten lava seeking a fissure to come to the top and explode through. Joseph had made overtures to Matt over the last couple of years, but Matt had not taken his father's efforts seriously. He did not seem to believe his father to be sincere and did not feel his father would make the time to carry through on any promises he might make.

Now, she hears from Cindy that Matt had recently been attacked in his own home and barely escaped with his life, and nobody knew why it happened or who the attacker was. Cindy had also informed her that Matt had taken Kelli and some friends on a trip to the Bahamas aboard his boat to look into something his grandfather had talked to him about. That was over a week ago. This was all very worrisome and mysterious. And of course, Matt would never call his mother and tell her what was really going on because he did not want to worry her.

What he doesn't understand is that keeping me in the dark is far more frightening than knowing a fearful truth.

Joseph had just confessed to her that he helped Matt out of a bad situation a couple of days earlier but couldn't elaborate further because it involved using classified NASA systems.

What in God's green earth could be going on in Matt's life that would require help from NASA? This was just getting to be too much for a mother's heart to take!

Carol took some comfort in the fact that Cindy and Ken were enjoying a relatively normal life and had raised two wonderful young men, Gavin and Gage, who would soon be off to college. They were twins and had been nicknamed "Double Trouble" from an early age. But mothers always worry about the ones who are not doing so well, even if all the others are fine. It's their job.

She refocused her attention to the task at hand and found a fuchsia-colored outfit with white piping down the sides. She really liked it, and the color would look good with her tan, which she maintained with great care and diligence. The outfit was in her size and on the sale rack, so she grabbed it and headed to the checkout. She paid for it with her debit card and waited while the clerk carefully folded and placed it in a flat bottom shopping bag. She accepted her receipt and headed to the parking lot where her pearl-white SUV was waiting. The White Stallion she called it.

Carol was deeply immersed in family thoughts as she put the bag in the rear cargo compartment of the car. She shut the hatch and squeezed in between her car and a white van parked alongside. *Someone could have done a better job of parking and left me a little space to get in my door,* she thought to herself. Selfish people.

Carol pressed the unlock button on her key fob and just as she was reaching for the handle on her car door, the side door panel of the van flew open, and two men in full-face masks grabbed her, quickly placing a gloved hand over her mouth while pulling her inside the interior of the van. Her heart pounded out of her chest, and she kicked wildly while trying desperately to scream for help. But the screams were stifled beneath the leather of the gloved hand that tightly covered her mouth and sounded no louder than a kitten's squeak. The masked men hurriedly slid the door shut again, slapped two strips of duct tape over her mouth, secured her wrists and ankles with plastic cable ties, and the driver slowly and quietly exited the parking lot as to not attract unwanted attention.

CHAPTER 10

Safe House
Johnson's Ridge, Kentucky

EVERYONE WAS SETTLING IN at the safe house. Ghost's rowdy relatives had shared a beer with them and headed on home. Ghost insisted that Matt and Kelli use the master bedroom while he and Jake took the two smaller bedrooms. The log home was a sturdy but comfortable space with all the modern conveniences that one could want—and more. There was a host of security measures in place, including a panic room underground that could be accessed by a trapdoor in the living room floor that was hidden under a large ornate rug with a Native American pattern woven into it. Built into a wall in the master bedroom closet, there was a combination safe that was large enough to hold the relics, and with Ghost's permission, Matt deposited them there. Ghost shared the combination with Matt, just in case.

Recessed into one of the great room walls was a locked gun safe with a wide assortment of rifles, assault weapons, and handguns. Next to the gun safe was a large floor locker constructed of the same wood that was used in the construction of the interior of the cabin. Ghost unlocked it and lifted the lid, revealing an array of flash bang and frag grenades, anti-personnel mines, various types and calibers of ammunition, night vision gear, knives, radios, and other lethal toys for that special occasion when only the best will do.

After viewing this impressive array of weaponry, gadgetry, and firepower, Jake whistled and said, "Well, I'm impressed, old friend. You could start a war with all the stuff you have up here."

"Or maybe stop one," Ghost replied with a slight smile.

"Good point. Depends which side you're on, I guess. You might want to show us the location of your trip alarms and other goodies, so we don't stumble into them during our vacation here and have everybody on this ridge, including your crazy relatives, ready to go to war. Just sayin'."

Ghost grinned. "No problem. Check this out."

Ghost opened the pantry door and taped to the inside of the door was a detailed grid of the various alarms and their placement around the property. The alarm locations were color-coded for iden-tification by type.

"Some of those are trip alarms that are always active, and the others are proximity alarms that I can turn on or off from inside the house. The control panel is over here," Ghost said, closing the pantry door.

"Where?" Jake asked.

"Right here."

Ghost walked over to the entertainment center that housed the large flat-screen TV, pushed firmly on the right side of it causing it to release and gently swiveled it around on its base. This revealed a communications center built into the backside of the entertainment center that controlled not only the proximity alarms but also featured satellite communications controls and radio monitors. Ghost then rotated the entertainment center back into its original position, picked up the remote control, and turned it on. A robust satellite TV lineup appeared on the screen.

"Uh … Ghost … I appreciate your hospitality, but I'm not ready to pop popcorn and watch a movie just yet," Jake said.

"I think you'll enjoy watching this channel," Ghost replied with a slight smirk and a twinkle in his eyes. He was thoroughly enjoying showing off his handiwork to his old partner.

He changed the input selection on the TV to an alternate slot, and the screen came to life with multiple camera views of the entire property.

"I have placed security cameras at strategic points all around the area, including the front gate. We can monitor anyone or anything approaching this house from about a mile out. In fact, I have a long-range 360°-view camera mounted on the top of the chimney that can see all the way to the main road. I don't like surprises or uninvited guests."

"Yeah, I can see that. It seems we both prefer to give surprises rather than get them," Jake said.

"And if we need manpower, my cousins can be here in minutes. I keep them on speed dial, and they're always up for an adventure."

"Jesus, Ghost! You must have spent a fortune on all this stuff," Matt said. "How much *did* they pay you guys in special ops?"

"Not as much as you might think," Ghost replied. "But operatives like Jake and I were always on the move, and the government covered all our expenses. My paychecks went mostly into savings and investments over the years. It added up. That's probably how Jake got his money for the marina and how I afforded all this."

"That would be a correct assumption, Pardner," Jake added.

"You never get rich working for the Shop, but some of the fringe benefits are excellent," Ghost continued. "It's going to be dark soon, and I'm gettin' hungry. I had the boys stock some fresh food in the house before we got here, so there's plenty to eat. Anybody up for some ribeyes on the grill?"

That offer was met with an enthusiastic response, and Ghost walked out on the back deck to start the gas grill. The deck was long and fairly wide, covered by the overhang of the roof, and running about half the length of the back of the house. Beyond it, there was a cliff that dropped almost straight down.

Matt's sat phone buzzed.

Matt answered, figuring it was Ken checking up on them. He was right about Ken being on the other end, but not about the purpose for the call. He put it on speaker so everyone could hear.

"Matt, Ken here. You guys alright?"

"Sort of. We all made it out of Bimini except Lucien. Those murdering bastards executed him right in front of us."

There was a pause on the other end of the line. They could all hear Ken curse quietly under his breath. After a few moments, Ken continued.

"I'm sorry to hear that. I really am. How did you get out of there safely?"

"I had no choice but to let Jake call in some favors from his old employer. They arranged transport back to the mainland. They sent a big seaplane right to our boat, of all things, and flew us to Homestead where we spent the night. From Florida, we flew to a safe house in another state where we are now. Jake also arranged to have Lucien's body shipped back home where his family could give him a decent funeral."

"I'm really sorry to hear about Lucien, but I'm glad the rest of you made it out in one piece. Are you able to tell me where you are?"

"I would like to, but I'm not sure how secure this sat phone connection is, and I can't take the chance that somebody is listening in on this call. They could be monitoring my sat phone since I've used it several times."

"Understood. I know it's been a rough couple days, but it's about to get rougher I'm afraid. Were you able to secure the items you were looking for?"

"Yes, we did, but what do you mean it's about to get rougher?"

"They have your mother, Matt."

You could hear the air go out of the room at that pronouncement. Everyone held their breath.

"Who's got my mother? What the hell are you talking about?"

"My guess is it's the same group that's been chasing you all along. They kidnapped Carol earlier today and sent me a text message with ransom demands and a picture of your mother in restraints. I guess they think I'm the most likely person to be able to contact you. I tried to trace the text to its source, but it was a burner phone, and I'm sure they've already disposed of it."

Matt was stunned. He could not believe what he was hearing. *Oh, my God! Not my mother. What have I done … ?*

"What are they asking for, Ken?"

"The relics."

CHAPTER 11

Kennedy Space Center
Deputy Director Flannery's Office

"Damn it, Ken! Who in the hell are these people? Why isn't someone doing something? Is Carol alright?"

"As far as I know, Joseph. She looked unharmed in the picture they sent. We don't know who these people are, but I'm pretty sure it's the same group that's been after Matt."

"What is it they want? If they hurt my Carol …"

"I know. Believe me, I know. We all feel the same way. Cindy's a mess and is here in the office with me. We're on my secure line. It seems they want to trade Carol for some relics Matt discovered on North Bimini."

"What the hell *are* these things and why are they so important that people are killing and kidnapping to get their hands on them?"

"Honestly, I don't have the answer to those questions. The last Matt and I discussed the matter he didn't know either. But he probably has a better idea of why they're so valuable now that he's found them."

"Ken, this is his mother we're talking about! Why doesn't he turn those things over to these crazy bastards so they will release her?"

"Knowing Matt, I'm sure he's struggling with those same decisions as we speak. I notified him of his mother's kidnapping and the ransom demand just a few minutes ago. One of his partners on the trip to Bimini was executed right in front of them, and the rest of them barely escaped with their lives—on several occasions, actually. He still has not told me what the importance of these relics might be, but evidently, they are important enough that he and his friends have repeatedly risked their lives to safeguard them."

"Holy Mother of God … what is happening here? He must believe these items are national security concerns or something similar, or he would not be risking his life and those of Kelli and his friends over it?"

"That's very possible. All I know is that your father knew enough about the value of these artifacts that he told nobody but Matt about them. Not even you or his wife. Neither did his partner, Mr. Bart, other than his grandson Lucien who was murdered on Bimini."

"What archeological discovery could possibly be that valuable? I mean, this sounds insane! You think it's because they might be worth a lot of money?"

"Joseph, I think we both know Matt better than that. He wouldn't endanger anyone he cared about over money. On the surface, it does sound insane, and I know it's hard to accept without knowing the rest of the story. But I have to believe that Matt knows what he's doing, and there's a lot more to this than we know at this moment."

"Okay … I'm sure you're right. I'm just so frustrated and angry right now. I feel so helpless. So, what do we do next? We have to find a way to rescue Carol. They have kidnapped the wife of a NASA administrator, and that is serious stuff in the government's eyes. I think Matt should offer to turn those relics over to these people and get his mother out of there. We can deal with these thugs later and try to recover the damned relics then. I should be reporting this to the FBI right now!"

"You might want to talk to Matt about that first. Once you let the FBI know about the kidnapping and ransom demand, they will insist on knowing what these relics are and take them into custody as a negotiating tool. Matt says this must not happen under any circumstances."

"Well, how does he plan to find and rescue his mother if we don't call in the government agencies?"

"I'm not sure, but he has some impressive resources at his disposal."

"Like what?"

"Joseph … you need to call Matt right now and talk to him about this. You two need to work it out … *together.*"

CHAPTER 12

Safe House
Johnson's Ridge, Kentucky

MATT'S SAT PHONE RANG and he walked over and picked it up.

"Hello".

"Matt, this is Ken again. I just talked to your father and he is beside himself with your mother missing. He doesn't understand why you don't just turn over those relics to these crazy people so you can get your mother released?"

"I have to find another way, Ken. I can't allow these murdering thieves to get their hands on these artifacts."

"What have you found, Matt? Why is it so important? Is it a matter of national security?"

"I can't divulge that information over this phone, but I will tell you that what I discovered has the means to rewrite history and the balance of power in this world … forever. It's that big."

"Okay, I will keep it under wraps … for now. But I have to call your father after I finish talking to you. He will want to call in the cavalry. What do you want me to tell him?"

"Tell him … to call me."

The sat phone buzzed. Matt regarded it like a gator that would bite off his arm if he picked it up. Things were never easy between him and his father.

"Hello."

"Matt … is that you?"

"Yes."

"This is your dad. Good to hear your voice, son. I understand you have lost a friend and survived some close calls. I'm sorry to hear about your companion."

"Surviving some close calls would be the understatement of the year at this point, but I appreciate the sentiments. I hear you hijacked a satellite to help me out. Appreciate it."

"Listen, I know things could be better between us, but we have to figure out what to do about this situation with your mother."

"I'm working on it."

"Matt, you know that all I have to do is let the director of NASA know about this, and the resources of the entire intelligence community will be brought to bear. They won't take kindly to having the wife of a NASA administrator kidnapped and held for ransom."

"I'm aware of that, Dad. And, I know how hard it must be for you to have hesitated even this long. It's damned hard for me too, quite honestly. I couldn't bear it if anything happened to Mom. But I have to ask that you give me a chance to use *my* resources to rescue Mom. I can't let the government know about the discovery I made. Nobody can be trusted with it."

"You're asking a lot, son."

"I know I am. I need you to trust me on this one."

"May I ask what it is you have found that is worth risking your life and that of your mother's over?"

"I can't talk about it over this unsecure connection, but trust me, it's that important. I didn't know how big it was until I actually found it."

"Do you think your grandfather knew?"

"I think he knew enough. That's why he never turned it over to the university or published his findings."

"Why do you think he chose you to see it through?"

"He trusted me, Dad. Something you need to do right now."

Joseph felt that statement hit him right in the gut. This was going to be an important moment in their relationship.

"Alright Matt, I trust you. I will hold off for now, but only for a little while. Keep me updated, please. Your mother means the world to me …"

"I know, Dad. Me too. Talk to you soon."

Matt had allowed the conversation to be heard by everyone in the room through the external speaker on the sat phone. He looked into the faces of these people who had been through so much with him in such a short time. Their faces reflected the emotions rolling around inside of him—anger, frustration, and concern for his mother's well-being as well as compassion for Matt.

"I talk a big game, but I don't even know how to start to find Mom. We can't trace the text message. The phone was a throwaway. Dad told Ken that he thinks they grabbed her in Cocoa Beach while she was shopping. But they could be holding her anywhere by now. I'm at a dead end. Maybe I should just turn over the relics to these ruthless bastards, hope they don't hurt Mom and try to recover them later."

The room was silent, everyone lost in their thoughts as they racked their brains for a solution to this quandary. Kelli sat next to Matt, squeezing his hand. Jake stared intently at the sat phone Matt had laid on the coffee table in the great room. He looked up at Matt.

"Matt, I have a bold plan if you have the nerve to see it through."

"Out with it, Jake. No time to beat around the bush here. I'm pretty sure we'll be getting a deadline message from these assholes before long."

"Without a doubt, you *will* be hearing from them soon. Okay, so here's what I'm thinking …"

CHAPTER 13

Dominion Winter Estate
West Palm Beach, Florida

Jordan Dominion leaned back in his imported leather desk chair and surveyed the magnificent woodwork and art that covered the walls of his eight-hundred-square-foot den. He thought about the workmen who had painstakingly created such a beautiful space—the rows of bookshelves and the untold years of toil and effort it had taken to write the books that lined the shelves, the rich cherry-wood paneling, the mirror-like polished wooden floor, and the hand-worked metal ceiling. He deeply appreciated the attention to detail and the desire for perfection that was displayed all around him. He shared these same traits with the anonymous craftsmen. His secure cell phone chimed, stirring him from his musings.

"Dominion here. Report."

"It is Kabil, sir. The mission is underway and has been executed flawlessly."

"Does that mean that our guest is in your custody?"

"Yes, sir. We took custody of the guest without incident."

"Is it possible you were seen by anybody?"

"No, sir. There were no observers nearby."

"How about security cameras on the buildings?"

"There were a couple, but my men were masked, and we had the capture vehicle crushed at a salvage yard immediately after the mission was completed. Nothing to see on the security footage that would help them."

"Have you sent the proof of equity and ransom demand to Mr. Spader?"

"Yes, we have. We destroyed the phone that was used, per your instructions, and we will employ a different one when we set the deadline and ask for acknowledgment from Mr. Spader."

"Good. I am pleased, Mr. Kabil. Is our equity unharmed?"

"Yes, sir. There has been no reason to harm our guest as of yet. But, should they refuse our demands, we will have to forward pictures of her in a … how should I say it … less comfortable state."

"I agree. However, I am considering a change of plans. My intelligence network has identified the signature of the satellite phone that Matt Flannery has been using. He used it several times over the last few days which allowed us to start a trace on it. Mr. Spader called it to speak with Mr. Flannery today. Another call was made to it as well by a party near Titusville, Florida. I assume that to be Mr. Flannery's father. My communications experts are very close to pinning down the origin of the sat phone transmissions on Mr. Flannery's end. This led me to think that we should change the game up a bit. Instead of working through a high-risk hostage negotiation, exchange, and having them come after us as would be the expectation, I propose we mount a surprise attack on their current location once identified and secure the relics. This would eliminate our need to make a hostage exchange and lessen our exposure. What do you think of my new plan, Mr. Kabil?"

"Excellent thinking, Mr. Dominion! This is a fortuitous development indeed!"

"Very well. As of now, this will be our primary plan. I will put my private jet on standby, and you will assemble an assault team to be ready on my command. This may be the break we have been waiting for. I do not believe they will be expecting this to happen which will tilt the odds heavily in our favor. In fact, I believe they will still be waiting for our next demand call when we hit them. I will have my experts continue to monitor the sat phone signal, and as soon as they have pinpointed its origin, I will text you the coordinates."

"We will be ready within the hour, Mr. Dominion. My people have extensive experience fighting house to house and hand to hand if necessary. They are well suited to this type of operation."

"A word of warning. Do not become overconfident. Thirty of your predecessors lost their lives to this little band of overachievers due to their overconfidence and lack of preparation. Do not make the same mistake. You have witnessed the price of failure."

"Understood, sir. We will be careful, but surprise will be on our side. *They will never see it coming.*"

CHAPTER 14

Safe House
Johnson's Ridge, Kentucky

"HERE'S WHAT I THINK we should do," Jake began. "I believe the sat phone is a tool we can use to turn the tables on these kidnappers."

"How can the sat phone help us?" Matt said. "If anything, it has probably become a liability since it's not a secure connection."

"Exactly," Jake replied. "The fact that it is *not* a secure connection could work in our favor. I believe with the resources our attackers have at their disposal, they will have the ability to locate and trace this sat phone signal. The fact that we have used it as often as we have almost guarantees that they have located the phone's location or soon will."

"Great. How in hell's blazes is that good news for us?" Matt asked.

"Think about it. Don't we always prefer to play offense instead of defense?"

"Yeah, we do. You've made me a believer."

"Okay then, here's the deal. I'm betting that if their operatives have any combat field experience at all, and I'm sure they do, they will think like I do. If they're able to trace the sat phone signature back to here, they will try to launch a surprise attack against us. If they can capture the relics straight out, they'll be able to avoid a hostage swap and all the risk that goes with it. If I were them, that is exactly what I would do. I think you should turn that sat phone on for a few minutes at a time and let the signal act as a beacon for them to follow. Dial up your home phone or mine or somewhere you know there won't be an answer and let it ring quite a few times before hanging up. I bet they'll follow those breadcrumbs like Hansel and Gretel."

"Alright, I'll buy your theory. But can we defend against a strong assault?"

"I will defer to Ghost on this one. He's the master of this domain."

"How many enemy combatants do you think we should prepare for, Jake?" Ghost asked.

"Hard to say, but I would expect at least eight or ten."

"Sounds about right. A larger force would be too conspicuous, and a smaller force might be considered insufficient considering their track record against us so far. They might be a little overconfident again since they will assume they possess the element of surprise. I think we can defend very effectively against a force that size. I will arm all warning systems, and we can place anti-personnel mines in strategic locations. You notice there is a loft with lots of windows in this house. That was by design. We will have a 360°-degree field of fire from up there. There is also a long drop off behind the house where the deck is. We won't have to worry about defending that side of the house unless they bring mountain climbing equipment. My guess is they will not. They will try to use speed and surprise against us. I also have one very special secret weapon in my back pocket that they will not account for."

"A Cobra gunship with optical gunsights?" Jake quipped.

"No, not a Cobra. Fort Knox is not that far, but I don't think we can get authorization for that in time to help us," Ghost replied with a grin. "But this is almost as lethal. Remember my crazy cousins? Those guys know these ridges and my property like the back of their hand. They have been coon hunting in the dark out here their whole lives. They are superior marksmen and are always up for a good fight if the situation calls for it, and this would qualify in their minds. We take care of our own up here. I like our chances."

"What do you think, Matt?" Jake asked.

"It sounds like a good plan, and it's the best shot we have right now to stop this on our own. But I have one more question, and it's an important one. If they come here and we take them down, what happens to my mother?"

"I've been thinking about that, too. Think your dad would be able to get us access to more satellite observations from earlier today?" Jake asked with a twinkle in his eye.

"He's pretty motivated at this point. He would do anything to bring Mom home. Tell me what you need, and I'll call him," Matt replied.

"Okay, but use my secure phone this time," Ghost said.

"Secure line?" Matt asked. "How do you get a secure satellite phone connection? I know you two know people in high places, but I thought you were retired?"

Ghost looked at Jake, and they both chuckled. "Retired? You can go inactive, but you can never retire," Ghost said.

"Kind of like being in the mob," Jake added. "You're in for life."

CHAPTER 15

"I HAVE A CALL for you from your son, Mr. Flannery. He has requested that you take it on a secure line."

"Thank you. Put it through immediately on a secure connection."

"Right away, sir."

Joseph Flannery quickly picked up the secure phone handset. His hands were sweating and a little shaky. *Please God … let this be good news.*

"What's your plan, Matt?"

"I think we have figured out a way to find Mom. Do you have 24/7 satellite surveillance of the Kennedy Space Center and surrounding area?"

"Yes, of course, we do. We are a highly classified area with a no-fly zone. Damn! Why didn't I think about that?"

"Don't worry about it, Dad. Somebody who is highly trained in this stuff thought of it, not me. We need you to obtain any aerial surveillance tapes of the Cocoa Beach area where Mom was shopping this morning. All you have to do is look for her car, where she parked it, and what type of vehicle she was taken away in. Once you have that vehicle ID'd, you can track it through various highway camera systems to its destination or at least close to it. If they didn't take her far from Cocoa, you might even have the vehicle's entire route on your tapes."

"Alright Matt, I can do that. I'm sure we have Cocoa Beach on our tapes and much of the surrounding area. Our surveillance cameras are very high resolution, and we can zoom in on an image with great clarity."

"That's good, Dad. I figured as much. It is NASA, after all. Let me know what you find. Thanks again for your help."

"Son, you don't have to thank me for helping save your mother's life. I don't know what all you're involved in at this point, but I want you to know that I trust you completely. Just like your grandfather did. He was just better at letting you know it than I was."

Matt was taken aback by this sudden show of faith and affection from his father. It thawed him out just a little inside and left him unsure of how to respond.

"Uh … I appreciate you saying that, Dad. Don't worry. We'll get Mom back. Call me on this secure line as soon as you get a look at those tapes."

"Will do. Talk to you soon."

The Deputy Administrator terminated the call and immediately dialed up the personal cell phone of the Director of Security for the Kennedy Space Center.

"Don Waller speaking."

"Don, Joseph Flannery here. This is a priority request, and I don't have time for an explanation. I need all aerial and street-level surveillance of the Cocoa Beach area for the last several hours, beginning about 0900. Consider this time-critical and link it to my computer terminal the first moment you recover the tracking footage."

"Of course, Mr. Flannery. Consider it done."

Don Waller ended the call and punched in a new number and pushed the call button.

After a couple of rings, it was answered.

"Dominion here. Why are you calling me directly?"

"We have a problem, Mr. Dominion."

CHAPTER 16

Dominion Winter Estate
Palm Beach, Florida

"Very well, Mr. Waller. We will push the timeline of our operations as much as possible. However, I do not expect it to be a problem in the end. We have a strategy to resolve this little problem without having to use the hostage."

"That's good to hear, Mr. Dominion. Mrs. Flannery is a very nice lady."

Jordan laughed heartily into the phone receiver.

"Her well-being means nothing to me, Mr. Waller. Sentiment is for weak-minded people. It has never been my intention to release her alive, even if the ransom was met. Loose ends annoy me, Mr. Waller. The dead see nothing and say nothing. You just make sure you do not arouse suspicion with Joseph Flannery. Go ahead and give him the tapes he has requested. By the time he pulls the information he needs from them, it will be too late to make use of it. By the way, you did a good job of keeping me informed on this matter. There will be a little something extra waiting in your bank account."

"Thank you, Mr. Dominion."

Jordan picked up his other cell phone and placed a call.

"Yes, sir."

"I have the coordinates for you, Amir."

"Excellent, sir."

"Are your men ready?"

"They are."

"I will text you the coordinates of your objective as soon as we finish our conversation. The jet is fueled and ready, and I have instructed the pilots to bring detailed topographical maps of the area you will be going to. The pilot will insert you at a landing strip near Lexington, Kentucky, that is owned by a wealthy horseman who no longer uses it. It is about a two-hour drive from the landing strip to your target destination. I will have SUVs waiting at the landing site for your men and their gear. Any questions?"

"No, sir."

"Very well. Check in with me when you are on the ground and again when you are ready to initiate your operation at the target location."

"I will, sir."

"I assume you are going to approach the target tonight?"

"Yes, we are."

"How many men are you taking with you?"

"Nine, sir. Ten counting me."

"Bring me those relics, Mr. Kabil."

"I will bring you the relics … or die trying."

"Good answer. Dominion out."

CHAPTER 17

Aboard the Dominion Private Jet

AMIR KABIL SURVEYED THE good men around him. These were his brothers-in-arms who were hand-picked by him for this mission. They were battle-tested, fearless, and reliable. He had fought alongside every one of them at different times and places but always for the same cause—holy jihad.

He allowed himself a slight smirk as he thought about how he had outsmarted the mighty Mr. Dominion. Did Dominion really think Amir would recover these valuable items, whatever they are, and just hand them over to him? Never. He would sell them on the black market for the best price he could get. He would use the funds to finance their continuing jihad and pay his men well for their loyal service to him and the cause.

Amir let his head sink back into the plush headrest and allowed his mind to relax just for a few moments. He might even save an explosive device for the pompous Mr. Dominion. The thought made him smile.

CHAPTER 18

Safe House
Johnson's Ridge, Kentucky

PREPARATIONS FOR THEIR DEFENSE were well underway. Ghost had called in his cousins, and they, along with everyone else in the house, were gathered around the big picnic table on the rear deck.

Ghost produced a detailed map of his property that showed all the hills, valleys, roads, and streams that surrounded his house. Ghost meticulously marked the locations of his alarms and surveillance cameras. There were no blind spots on the road leading to the house as cameras covered the entire length of it. The main gate was locked and secured as well. There was little chance the attackers would be careless enough to make a direct assault through the main gate, so Ghost turned his attention to the other, less obvious ways to reach his cabin.

"Jake," Matt said, "how sure are you that they'll wait to attack after dark?"

"Close to a hundred percent sure. We have to allow time for them to organize and travel here, which should take the rest of the day. Only total amateurs would try to sneak back in here during daylight, and they will not send amateurs. They have to believe the most powerful weapon they possess right now is stealth and surprise. I guarantee you they believe we're sitting up here, snug as bugs in a rug, waiting on the ransom phone call and expecting nothing to happen before that. So, I don't see them making any bonehead moves that would compromise their element of surprise. I say it will definitely be a night operation."

"Makes sense. Do you think they could come as early as tonight?"

"Absolutely. I would. In their minds, the longer they wait, the less chance they have of catching us off guard. Tonight is their optimum window of operation. I'm pretty sure the breadcrumbs we left them on the sat phone are sufficient for them to have traced us here, and we know they have the resources to get assets airborne and in position within hours. So, I'm betting that tonight it is."

"Well, whether it happens tonight or not, we have to prepare as if it will," Ghost stated. "Since we agree they will not likely try an open daylight assault, let's look at the other ways they could approach our position. The backside of the house is pretty secure with the cliff acting as our protection on that side. I do have proximity alarms on that cliff, just in case. They will probably look for some paths through the woods to make their advance quieter and quicker than hacking through brush and undergrowth. There are paths. They are all marked here on the map. By design, there are only two for them to choose from. One runs back here from the main highway and parallels the entrance road to the cabin. The other path enters off the highway further back and leads through a small creek and gulley before climbing up the ridge where the house sits. We need to secure those two trails and place anti-personnel mines off to the side should they break and run when confronted. I have already asked my cousins to let all the neighbors know there could be some noise up here tonight and not to worry about it or call the police. Actually, one of the neighbors down the road *is* the police, as well as my uncle, and he said to let him know if we need help. Otherwise, he agreed to look the other way. So, let's break out the mines and night vision gear to prepare a welcoming party for our uninvited guests. You know how much I hate uninvited guests …"

CHAPTER 19

Abandoned Air Strip
Near Mount Sterling, Kentucky

THE AIRSTRIP HAD NOT been used in a couple of years and was in less than ideal condition, but still adequate for Dominion's private jet to make a safe landing. Amir Kabil and the nine operatives who accompanied him hurried down the stairs that extended forth from the plane. They pulled their collars up against the cold north wind that bit into their skin. They looked around for the vehicles that were supposed to meet them and saw the parking lights of two large, black SUVs sitting off to the side at the end of the runway, outlined in the landing lights of the jet. The drivers turned on their headlights and brought the vehicles alongside the aircraft where the operatives were waiting along with their lethal gear. Amir and four of his men loaded into the lead vehicle, and the other five climbed into the second one. Amir took the front passenger seat so he could direct the operation from there. He checked his radio, and the team leader in the second vehicle signaled he had strong reception.

Amir turned his attention to the driver. He looked to be in his forties and an American. Probably not trustworthy in his estimation. He then addressed the driver.

"What are your orders?"

"To pick you up at this location, and you would give me further instructions at that time."

"Excellent. Do not move the vehicle until I give the order. Please roll down your window so I can hear everything that is occurring outside this car."

The driver complied and waited, eyes forward.

Amir pressed the talk button on his shoulder-mounted radio again and waited for his other team leader to respond.

"Yes?"

"We are now taking full command of this operation. Proceed as planned."

"Understood."

In one practiced movement, Amir drew his handgun and fired a deadly round into the temple of the doomed driver. Blood and fleshy matter sprayed across the driver's side of the vehicle as the bullet exited the other side of the driver's head and through the open window. As the man slumped over the wheel, Amir turned to look out the back window of the SUV where he saw the flash and heard the pop of a shot being fired in the trailing vehicle. Amir slid out of the passenger seat and briskly walked back to the passenger side of the other SUV. After confirming that the second driver was dead as well, he praised the team leader for his efficiency and loyalty.

Amir believed the drivers had it coming to them anyway. He justified his actions by telling himself they were infidels in the eyes of Allah and worked in the service of their godless employer, Dominion.

The team leader swung out of the passenger side door and walked around the front of the SUV to the driver's side and dragged the driver out of the seat and to a spot off to the side of the runway. He then returned to the SUV and rummaged around the interior until a polishing cloth was found under a seat. He used the rag to wipe down the driver's door, and once the human debris had been cleared, the team leader took his position behind the wheel.

Amir returned to the lead vehicle, where his team had already removed the dead driver, laying him alongside the other corpse on the side of the runway. Amir's team stripped the dead man of his shirt and used it to clean up the mess resulting from the execution of the driver. One of the operatives removed a spare gasoline can from the back of the lead SUV, carried it over to where the two dead bodies lay in the darkness, and soaked both of them thoroughly with the highly flammable fuel. The operative then used a lighter to ignite the gasoline and watched with an air of detachment as both bodies were quickly engulfed in flames. Amir had requested a container of gasoline be stored inside the SUV in advance of the assault team's arrival in anticipation of what events would transpire on the dark, remote runway. It was all part of his ruthless plan.

Amir watched the shadowy scene play out, showing and feeling no emotion. *Dead men don't talk. What does the death of two insignificant infidels matter to me? What loss are they? Millions more like them will die before the jihad is finished. Praise be to Allah!*

He signaled a thumbs-up to the pilots of the jet who had been watching the grisly drama unfold, indicating that it was time for them to get airborne. They were to move the Dominion jet to nearby Blue Grass Airport at Lexington for refueling, then standby for the signal to extract the team at this same location once the mission had been completed.

But Amir had his own plans for the pilots and the plane.

The commandos were now ready to advance to their objective, and Amir chose to drive the lead vehicle. He plotted the coordinates of their destination into a sophisticated handheld GPS unit, and the black vehicles sped off into the night. As he drove away from the runway area, Amir glanced at his rearview mirror, where he could see the gleaming jet powering up for takeoff. The funeral pyre of the dead men reflected off the fuselage in a flickering, ghostly play of light. Amir sneered as he imagined how the flames of hell would be engulfing those stupid men right now. *They will feel the wrath of Allah for eternity!*

He turned his full attention to the dark road in front of him. He felt invincible and self-righteous. The operation was on schedule, and the assault would begin after midnight.

CHAPTER 20

GHOST AND JAKE WERE busy distributing automatic weapons, sidearms, comm units, and night vision gear to everyone in the cabin. Perry and the other cousins had brought their hunting rifles, but Ghost persuaded them that switching to assault rifles might be a better idea since the enemy would certainly be equipped with them.

There had been a heartfelt attempt by Matt, Ghost, and Jake to convince Kelli to take up a position in the safe room and sit this one out. But, as usual, Kelli would have none of it. In fact, she tried to talk them into letting *her* take the point on one of the trail defense teams. She argued that she was small and fast and would be hard to detect. That offer did not fly with the group of protective males in the room, so they came up with a compromise.

Jake persuaded her to monitor the security camera feeds and central communication center, acting as home base for everyone in the field. She would also be the last line of defense should the bad guys make it all the way to the cabin. Should that unthinkable event occur, she was to open the secure line to Joseph Flannery and tell him to immediately enlist the authorities to rescue Carol and then call the police and request emergency assistance to their Johnson Ridge location. After accomplishing those tasks, she was to hide in the safe room with the relics until help arrived.

Perry Johnson and the three cousins were assigned to defend the paths through the woods because of their familiarity with the terrain. They would split up and put two men on each of the two trails that led to the homestead. Jake would take up a sniper position in the loft of the cabin where he could pick off anyone that made it through the outer defenses. Matt would stay near the house to add another layer of protection and provide backup for Jake while watching over Kelli. Ghost was going to be Ghost. He would disappear into the woods and wreak havoc on anyone he could. Everyone wore night vision goggles and had night scopes on their assault weapons. An assortment of handguns and concussion grenades were distributed to the defenders as well as lethal combat knives. The home team was as ready as they were going to get.

It was well past dark when they took up their positions, checked in with each other on the comm units, and settled in for the waiting *… waiting to spring the jaws of their trap.*

CHAPTER 21

Assault Team Staging Area
Johnson's Ridge, Kentucky

Amir and his team hid the SUVs inside a gray, derelict tobacco barn covered with a sagging, rusty metal roof. There were holes in the aging, weathered siding large enough to throw a cat through as the old-timers in the hills were fond of saying. The barn was situated on an abandoned homestead that had likely belonged to a tobacco farmer in years past. The location was ideal. It offered perfect cover for their vehicles and was a short hike away from the target destination. Amir could feel his adrenalin pumping as he looked around at his men.

"My brothers, this night, we will do a great thing. We will subdue our enemies, and we will take for ourselves a treasure the capitalist pig Dominion desires more than silver or gold. I have easily deceived him in the interest of our cause. We will not only take the treasure, but we will keep it for ourselves. Allah has provided us with this opportunity for a great victory! We will use the money to wage worldwide jihad and to support our longsuffering families back home."

One of the men asked a question. "Amir, you know we will follow you to the ends of the earth. But, may I ask what the treasure is? We don't even know what we are searching for."

"That is a good question, and it is time to share with you what I know, my brothers. We are here to find and secure a group of ancient artifacts. I have been told they are not large items but are valuable beyond our imagination. That is all I know at this time, but I can assure you that if Mr. Dominion has placed this much importance on stealing them, they must be worth a large fortune."

"Amir, if I may ask one more question, will Mr. Dominion not come after us with a vengeance? He is a powerful man, and his reach is very long."

"Be not concerned with Mr. Dominion, my friend. I have a plan to smuggle us out of the country as soon as we have secured the treasure. Once we board his private jet with the artifacts, we will force the pilots to take us out of the country. We will disappear before he knows what happened. Once we are back in our homeland, reunited with our families, our people will hide us and keep us safe. Now, put on the armor of holy warriors. Cover your faces and check your weapons. We must move swiftly and take our enemy by surprise. Tonight, we are the Sword of Allah! They will not see us coming, and we will strike with speed and vengeance. We will show no mercy to those who stand in our way. Allah is with us, so who can stand against us?"

"None can stand against us!" came the reply from the men.

"Form a double column, and we will follow the road staying close to the tree line. There is a trail about a mile down this road that will lead us through the woods and to the house where they are no doubt sleeping the sleep of the damned. Let's move quickly to our glorious destiny!"

CHAPTER 22

Hostage Holding Room
Location Unknown

CAROL'S EYES BLINKED OPEN, and she felt extremely groggy. She decided someone must have drugged her on the way to where she was now. She slowly surveyed the room where she was being held. It was bleak and unremarkable. There was a single window on one side of the room, but it was covered over with a thick blanket. Intruding through the wall, just below the window, was a noisy air conditioning unit. A 60s-era black pole lamp with tulip-like appendages held low wattage bulbs that provided the only light in the room. The tulips were pointed upward, and the light bulbs created dim halos on the ceiling. An old crushed velvet sofa covered with a floral throw stretched along one wall. Two sleeping bags stretched out on the floor. A small card table with two folding chairs held court in the middle of the musty room. The paint on the walls was a light yellow color mottled with rusty streaks caused by water leaking through a deteriorating roof and ceiling. The whole space smelled of sweat and mildew. The sweaty smell was emanating from two men sitting at the table playing cards. They were dressed in ominous black clothes and masks. There were two handguns and a cell phone lying on the table near their hands. Two long guns of some sort stood in the corner near the doorway leading to the rest of the house. Fast food containers lay scattered around the men's feet: chicken buckets and burger bags. A cooler at the end of the sofa was where they kept their drinks.

Carol glanced down at her personal accommodations. She was sitting in a natty, green, upholstered armchair with wooden arms and legs. Her arms were no longer secured to each other with wire ties but had been bound to the arms of the chair with nylon rope. Her ankles were secured to the legs of the chair with the same type of rope. Her mouth was still covered with a strip of duct tape. She had to pee really, really bad. She shook and rocked the chair so violently that it almost tipped over backward. She made all the noise she could through the tape over her mouth in an attempt to get the captors' attention. It worked.

Seeing that the woman was about to flip over, they jumped up and grabbed hold of the chair, putting it back on solid footing. Carol continued to squeal and make bug eyes at them, hoping they would remove the tape and allow her to speak. The two men looked at each other for a moment, and one nodded for the other to remove the tape from her mouth.

The man on her left stepped forward and painfully ripped the strip of tape from her face, soliciting a loud curse from the captive woman. She took a few deep breaths and tried to calm herself enough to speak.

"I really need to use the toilet!" Carol's voice was hoarse yet defiant.

"We have taken your physical needs into account."

"What does that mean? Are you going to let me use a bathroom or not?"

"Well, we decided that would be a lot of work on our part. Tying and untying you and escorting you to the bathroom, trying to make sure you don't do something foolish. So, we made a different plan that will be easy for you and easy for us."

"I suggest you share that plan with me pretty soon, or I will be making a mess all over this high-end piece of furniture you have me tied to!" Carol had been known to show her temper when someone rattled her cage, and being kidnapped had definitely rattled her cage. She was both scared and enraged.

"This will not be a problem, Mrs. Flannery. We want you to enjoy your stay with us, and hopefully, you will post a five-star review online after you leave our luxury hotel."

Both men laughed heartily at the joke, but Carol was not amused, and her bladder was screaming for relief. *Damn! I should not have had that third cup of coffee this morning! But then, I wasn't planning on being kidnapped either!*

"I appreciate your wonderful sense of humor, gentlemen, but I have to go to the bathroom NOW!"

"Okay, okay! Remain calm. Here is all you have to do to relieve yourself. Please raise your bottom off the seat for a moment."

"Why? That won't help. I need you to untie me and take me to a toilet!"

"Just do as we ask, and you will see."

"I will not! That won't help at all."

"Oh, but it will."

"How?"

"Let us show you how simple this will be."

With that, one of the men moved to the back of the chair and stood behind her. He reached through the space between her arms and her body and clasped his hands together just below her chest. He now tightened his arms around her in a big hug and pulled her upward. There was just enough slack in the ropes to allow her posterior and legs to raise up off the seat bottom. Carol was not sure what was going on but was nearing a state of panic as the captor manhandled her body.

"Now, please look beneath you."

Carol looked down between her thighs at the space under her rear and saw a hole had been cut out in the chair bottom and a plastic bucket placed underneath.

"What? You expect me to go like this? This is inhumane! And I don't want to sit in wet clothes when I'm done."

"Of course not! We would not want that for you either. Do you think us savages? You might get a rash!"

Both men laughed again and high-fived.

"I don't understand how this is supposed to work."

"Fortunately, you had the wisdom to wear a stretchy pair of slacks for your shopping trip today. You probably wanted to be comfortable. Am I right?"

"Yes. And?"

"That will make things work perfectly!"

The man behind her still had her suspended in the air above her seat, and now the man in front of her stepped forward and grabbed each side of her stretchy slacks and underwear and yanked them down to her knees, uncovering her private areas.

Carol shrieked and cursed and wiggled, but it was a useless exercise. She could not really control the situation, not even a little bit, and all the moving around was making it harder to hold it.

The man behind her lowered her down onto the seat, and she could now feel the hole in the chair beneath her and the cool air circulating up through it against her exposed bottom. The sensation of the air against her skin was the final straw. She could hold it no longer. Relief came quickly and noisily as the flood found the plastic bucket.

Then she remembered she was partially naked in front of these strangers and completely at their mercy. Fear bloomed in her stomach and rose into her chest, causing her eyes to widen as she looked up at the man in front of her.

The captor in front of her asked, "Finished?"

"Yes."

"Good! Now that wasn't so bad, was it?"

With that, the man in the back lifted her again, and the man in front approached her and reached toward her exposed body. Carol instantly recoiled as much as she could while still in restraints.

"What are you doing? You're not going to touch me down there, or anything, are you?"

The man in black stopped his advance and straightened slowly to his full height, putting both hands on his hips. He stared at her for a few moments as if considering what he should say next, then looked up at the man behind her, then looked back down at her. Having given it adequate thought, he answered her.

"No, woman, I am not going to violate you. We consider women in this country to be unclean and vulgar. We would not associate with females such as you where we come from."

"Oh. Well, that's good to know … I guess." Carol could not decide whether to be relieved or insulted.

"Besides, you are too old." That unwelcome remark came from the man who was behind her. Carol figured he could not make a statement like that while looking her in the eye, and if her hands were free, she would poke him in the eye.

"Too *old*? Too old for what, may I ask?" Carol responded in a peeved voice.

"Too old for young, virile men like us to be with … physically. You are old enough to be our mother."

"Well, maybe I am, but I can tell you that we vulgar, old women here in this country could teach a thing or two to those child brides you guys like to pluck up before their time. And, I would have taught you to show more respect to women if you were my sons!"

The man in front decided this conversation had gone on long enough and moved toward her again. He quickly pulled her slacks and underwear up to an acceptable position, and the man behind her lowered her back down to the seat, retracted his arms from under her armpits, and walked to the cooler. He pulled out a bottle of water and brought it to her, twisting off the lid and holding it to her raw, parched lips. A peace offering, she assumed. She took long, thirsty drinks from the bottle before he took it away.

"Thank you," Carol said quietly.

"We must keep you alive and healthy for now, Mrs. Flannery. Your son's refusal to give us the things we requested is the reason you find yourself here as our guest today. He will soon see the error in his thinking and come to his senses."

"I know my son, and if he has not given in to you, there is a very good reason for it."

"Oh yes, there is a *very* good reason why he has resisted us. But we are betting that he places more value on his mother's life than on those things he withholds from us."

"What are these things you want so badly from him?"

"Just some old relics. Hard to believe he would put his friends and family in danger because of them."

"Again, I know my Matt. If he's putting up a fight over this, there's a lot more to these relics than what you're telling me. One thing you must understand about my son—he will always do the right thing, even if that means putting himself and other people in harm's way. He's strong, and he's smart. You will not win if you continue to go up against him."

"Spoken like a true mother. I tire of her voice. Tape her mouth again."

CHAPTER 23

GHOST WAS FOCUSED ON monitoring his alarms and surveillance screens. His vigilance paid off.

"Alert 1, perimeter alarm has been tripped," Ghost whispered into his comm unit. "There has been a breach detected on Trail B where it leaves the highway. Unless a deer wandered onto the path, it seems our guests have arrived. Perry, move both your two-man fire teams into position on that path. I suggest you set up on the high ground where the path comes up out of the gulley. You'll have the strategic advantage from up there."

"On our way. We really hate trespassers around these parts," Perry answered as he spat on the ground.

"Listen up, everyone," Ghost continued. "Remember, our goal is to not only defend ourselves but to take a live prisoner. We need to find out who these attackers are and who they work for. You were all given wire ties to secure live captives, so use them. Try to avoid a full-on firefight if possible. Pick them off individually and bring them in alive if you can. Jake and I will get them to talk. I guarantee that. Good luck and stay in communication."

Ghost turned to Kelli and said, "Controls are all yours now, Captain." He ran out the front door into the night and disappeared … like a ghost.

CHAPTER 24

Amir's Assault Team
On Trail B
Johnson's Ridge, Kentucky

THE ENTIRE ASSAULT TEAM had switched to their night vision goggles and were making their way along the path that would lead them to their objective. They had made their way about two hundred yards into the woods when the trail sloped downward and descended into a shallow stream bed that looked to be dry. Amir held up his hand, signaling his men to stop.

Amir listened to the silence of the night. The forest was eerily quiet. It was a cold November evening. Dark, leafless trees reached out with their bony limbs toward the black sky. They were barely visible under the moonless heavens above. The colder temperatures meant fewer insects and other creatures stirring about in the night. He heard and saw nothing to be concerned about. Yet, this unnatural quiet was causing alarms to go off in his head. He was not sure why. *Too easy so far?*

He thought about it for a moment. They were moving into a low spot, which would be an ideal location should their enemies want to ambush them. All his forces were concentrated in one place, which was also risky. They were proceeding on the assumption they were not expected, but what if that was a faulty assumption? What if the enemy had deployed lookouts as a routine precaution? After all, these adversaries had demonstrated uncanny resilience and resourcefulness, time after time. Maybe he should take a more cautious approach.

Amir turned to his men and addressed the Team Two Leader.

"Do you remember the other path we saw on our maps?"

"Yes, Brother."

"Good. I am going to take Team One, return to the main road, and advance to the objective using that other path. You and your team will wait here until I signal you that we are moving up the second path. It would be wise if we split our force and attack on two fronts at the same time. If one of our squads is engaged, the other can still continue the mission."

"Wise decision as always, Amir."

Amir signaled his four-man squad to move out, and they headed back the way they came, quickly disappearing into the chilly night.

CHAPTER 25

Deputy Administrator Flannery's Office
Kennedy Space Center

JOSEPH FLANNERY PICKED UP his office phone and selected the secure line. It was a little past midnight, and he had to do something. He could no longer sit here and do nothing to help his Carol. He entered the phone number he was given to contact Matt's sat phone. The phone rang twice, and a female voice answered.

"Who is this?"

"I'm trying to reach Matt. Who is *this*?"

"Is this Mr. Flannery? This is Kelli."

"Hi, Kelli. Yes, it's me. Good to hear your voice. Can I speak to Matt? It's urgent."

"I'm afraid that's not really possible at the moment. We're in the middle of a pretty dicey situation. Can I have him call you back when it's over?"

"How long do you think it will be?"

"Not sure, Mr. Flannery. Could be an hour or longer depending on the outcome."

"The outcome of what? What's going on there, Kelli?"

"The bad guys discovered the location of our safe house and sent an assault team. They are on the ground here right now. We know where they are and have a good plan to defend ourselves, but I'm not sure how long this will take to play out."

"Jesus, Kelli! We have to stop all this craziness before someone else gets hurt or killed."

"I know. Believe me, I know. We're doing the best we can to stop these people. Is there any more news about Mrs. Flannery?"

"Nothing from the kidnappers, which seems odd to me. We should have received ransom demands or deadlines by now."

"Well, it could be they're waiting to see if this fishing expedition they sent our way is going to be successful before they try to use the hostage strategy. They won't need a hostage if they can get the relics tonight."

Kelli tensed as she realized what she had just said and the implications of her statement.

"Oh my God, Kelli. You're right. They might decide that even if they fail on your end, they have set themselves up for a fall and decide to dispose of Carol and move on. I know Matt wanted me to wait to contact the authorities, but I fear we're running out of time. I have to try to do something to save my wife, and I know that Matt is too engaged there to carry out his own plan to rescue his mother."

"If the government gets involved, you know they will come after Matt and all of us for questioning. They will also take possession of the artifacts, which is what we have been trying to avoid."

"Yes, I do know that. I'm sorry. I truly am. But the surveillance tapes that Matt advised me to look at told quite a tale. I was able to trace the kidnappers all the way to where I believe they are holding Carol at a location near Melbourne. I have to send somebody in before it's too late. If something happened to her because I didn't act quickly enough, well, I couldn't live with myself. I wouldn't want to."

"I understand, Mr. Flannery."

"Please, Kelli, call me Joseph."

"Okay, Joseph. I'll let Matt know you called as soon as this is over. I know he will want to talk to you."

"And Kelli, be safe and … let Matt know that I love him."

CHAPTER 26

Assault Team 1
Johnson's Ridge, Kentucky

AMIR KABIL AND HIS four team members followed the main road past the gravel driveway that led to the cabin in the woods. Only a few yards further down the highway, they discovered the second trail they were searching for. The squad quickly entered the trailhead with Amir in the lead. Once out of sight from the highway, he held up a closed fist as a signal to stop. He keyed the mic on his comm unit using two short bursts. After a moment, he received a reply of two clicks through his earbuds, signaling that Team Two had received his message and would now proceed to the objective.

He gave the thumbs-up signal to his unit, and they moved forward into the darkness, locked and loaded with deadly intentions.

CHAPTER 27

Safe House
Johnson's Ridge, Kentucky

"GHOST … THIS IS Base," Kelli said into the headset mic that was attached to her comm unit.

"Go ahead, Base."

"A proximity alarm has been tripped on Trail A out by the main road."

"Good work, Kelli. They must have split their force. Perry, do you read me?

"Loud and clear."

"I guess you heard the report from Kelli. They are now approaching on both trails. Can you get two of your guys back over to cover that other trail?"

"No can do. The two who were covering Trail A just arrived back here at my position to reinforce Trail B, and it would take too long for them to go back and get into position again on Trail A."

"Roger that. You four feel confident you can handle the five that are coming your way?"

"Piece of cake, Cuz. They won't know what hit 'em until it's too late. I've cornered raccoons meaner than these piss-ants."

"Don't get cocky, Perry. This won't be the first action these guys have seen. They're dangerous. Watch yourself and take care of the cousins."

"Will do. You guys just take care of those other five."

Ghost now turned his attention to defending Trail A.

"Jake, it looks like you and me are going to have to handle that group out on Trail A. You been following the chatter?"

"Affirmative. I heard it all. I'm coming down from my sniper position as we speak. I'll meet you at this end of the trail shortly."

"Roger that, Jake. Matt, you will be our last line of defense, so stay out of sight near the house and don't let anybody slip past you."

"I got your back, guys," Matt replied.

Kelli rejoined the conversation.

"Ghost, this is Base. The comm scanner you have in here is not only picking up our conversations but has picked up another frequency that is being used nearby. There has not been any chatter on it yet, but a few signals have been sent in the last few minutes."

"Good to know, Base. The two units are probably communicating with each other through comm clicks. Jake, on your way out here, pick up a spare comm unit so we can listen in on them. Kelli has the frequency."

"I'm in the house now, Pardner. See you in a short."

CHAPTER 28

Hostage Location
Melbourne, Florida

IT WAS WELL INTO the dark depths of the night, just past three a.m. Around twelve thirty, Joseph Flannery had alerted local law enforcement officials of the situation his wife was in and what he had found on the surveillance tapes. They asked about demands and deadlines, and he informed them he had not received either. He did not reveal the fact that this situation was linked to another taking place hundreds of miles away. He did not want to complicate the situation. He just wanted Carol returned home, safe and sound.

The SWAT team and hostage rescue team had been frantically assembled and were now in place. The team leaders were using high-powered night vision glasses to observe the aging, dilapidated, single-story shotgun house. It sat on about an acre of wooded land just outside the western city limits of Melbourne. There was a single light showing faintly through a window in a room facing the road, but it had been covered over, and the observers could not see inside. The rest of the windows in the house were shuttered, too, so the rescuers could not determine where the hostage was located within the structure and how many individuals were in there with her. There was an older model Chevy Trailblazer parked alongside the house, but no other vehicles.

The SWAT unit that had been dispatched to the scene was comprised of twenty men. It was made up of the most experienced, highly trained members of the local law enforcement agencies, many of them veterans with combat experience in the Middle East. Some of them had crawled into position in a 360-degree circle surrounding the house and property after stashing their vehicles well down the road and out of view of the hostage-takers. Additional officers and cruisers were in reserve about a half mile away. A couple of SWAT snipers had climbed into large trees on adjacent properties that afforded clear views of the two entry and exit points.

The SWAT team leader now deployed a FLIR heat-sensing camera that could make out heat signatures of bodies, even through the walls of a house. He trained the camera on the front side of the house, where the dim light had been observed. He moved it slowly back and forth, watching the bright colors on the screen dance and morph into different shapes and shades of red, orange, and yellow. He repeated the procedure several times to be sure of what he was seeing, then announced his findings to the hostage rescue team leader who was in charge of the overall operation.

"Sir, I detect a heat signature of two bodies in that front room nearest the street. Both are in a lying position on the floor and probably alive, given the amount of heat I see on their signatures. Maybe sleeping."

"Well, that's the best scenario we could hope for. We've pointed high sensitivity microphones at different places on the house, and we've picked up no voices or movement within the structure. Time to move in and see what we have here. Remember, instruct your SWAT guys not to get too gung-ho. The hostage is the wife of a top NASA official. We don't want any harm to come to her as a result of our actions here tonight. Understood?"

"Understood."

"Very well, move in on my command."

CHAPTER 29

Assault Team 2
Johnson's Ridge, Kentucky

"Isam, DO YOU THINK we will reach the house first and claim the glorious victory? Amir would be most proud of us!"

Isam, Leader of Team Two, stopped and looked back at the man following immediately behind him.

"Perhaps, my friend, perhaps. But we should not speak unless necessary, and we must remain vigilant. It is good that we have passed through this small valley without opposition, but we still must make it over this hill and through a wooded area before we can surprise the enemy who are in their soft beds believing they are safe. That is where they will die. Tonight, they will know that infidels and the unfaithful are never safe from our holy jihad. *Allah be with us.*"

The small group of five operatives began ascending the steep side of the ridge, finding it difficult to follow the narrow trail in the inky darkness, even with the help of their night vision glasses. They were nearing the top of the ridgeline when Isam raised a closed fist, signaling them to stop and catch their breath before pushing on to the objective. He felt excitement building in his stomach.

Soon, the treasure would be captured, their families would be wealthy, and they would be the new heroes of the jihad!

After a short rest, Isam led his team forward to the top of the hill. As he was about to place a foot on level ground again, he felt a movement in the darkness and looked up from the trail. He found himself staring straight into the barrel of an assault rifle.

Isam's battle experience had taught him not to make rash moves when encountering danger, but rather to stop and assess the situation. After all, he was responsible for his brothers behind him as well.

He slowly turned his head to the left where he could see another gunman had stepped out from behind a tree near the front of their column. He moved his eyes to the right and saw nobody. By now, the men behind him saw the two gunmen as well. The three operatives in the rear of the group decided retreat would be the best plan of action and turned to run back down the trail, assuming they would be hard to follow in the darkness.

Isam saw the gunman in front of him show his white teeth in a half-smile and then comprehended what he was smiling about. More defenders had appeared on the path behind his squad. The gunmen were commanding them to stop moving and had them covered with automatic weapons. The infidels had cut off their escape route, knowing that it would be hard to get away through the woods to the left or right because of the heavy undergrowth and trees. Isam could not believe his eyes. His mind was fumbling for an explanation.

How could they have known we would be here? The plan had been executed to perfection. Was there a traitor in their midst that had tipped them off?

Isam slowly turned his head again to face his adversary. The one with the big, white teeth and the grin of a devil.

"You have very nice teeth, sir," Isam offered in an effort to buy time and think.

"Why, thank you, Mr. Scumbag! I've always had a thing about my teeth. Damned dentist has cost me a fortune. Now, why don't you show me how smart you are and turn around and tell your fellow scumbags to lay down their weapons, nice and slow?"

"Please tell me, what is this 'scumbag' name you are calling me?" Isam asked.

"It's what you see every time you look in a mirror. I have other names I can call you that you might like better. Would you prefer Shithead?

"Well, I see you have us at a disadvantage, Mr. White Teeth. I do not understand these names, but I will do as you wish."

Isam turned around to face his brothers and began to formulate a desperate plan. Perry could see that Isam was stalling and might be thinking of doing something stupid.

"Uh … Mr. Scumbag … I don't know what is going through your pea brain right now, but I wouldn't try to be a hero if I was you. We have this area rigged with anti-personnel mines and other assorted goodies. I don't know if you have ever seen what one of those mines do to a human body, but it ain't pretty."

"I have seen the results from many of those mines you speak of. My home country is full of them."

"That's good. Then, you'll not be tempted to refuse my hospitality and make a run for it."

Isam knew that it was now or never. He did not believe Mr. White Teeth's story about having anti-personnel mines in the area. It was a convenient and easy way to maintain control of people through fear of the unknown—a tactic he had used successfully on many occasions. Isam was still facing to the rear in plain view of his men who had been bunched together behind him. He could see that four gunmen were guarding his team, and they were all cheated toward one side of the trail. That was a mistake he could exploit.

Isam spoke to his group in their native Iranian dialect and pretended to be telling them to lay down their arms but was actually instructing them to do something entirely different. On his signal, they were to make a break for the woods off to the side of the trail that was unguarded. They could work their way around to join up with Amir's squad and reinforce them.

Ha! Stupid Mr. White Teeth! You cannot fool me so easily.

Isam had been speaking in a low, even tone to not raise suspicion but now shouted in his most ferocious voice, *"Allah!"*

The men had been told this was the signal to break off into the woods. They half-ran and half-dove into the thickets on the less guarded side of the trail. For some reason, the gunmen had not fired upon them yet. *Perhaps they were afraid to pursue them!*

Perry shook his head and watched the men throw themselves headlong into the brush that bordered the south side of the trail. He looked over at his cousins and said, "Stupid asses … I tried to warn them." Perry was not the kind to bluff, except in poker.

Perry and his cousins quickly retreated even further to the north side of the path and watched the invaders thrashing through the undergrowth like madmen with their hair on fire. It did not take long for the still night to be shattered and lit up like the Fourth of July.

One ear-splitting explosion and then another crashed through the wooded valley. The accompanying bright white flashes of the mines being triggered briefly exposed the terrible carnage being inflicted on the invaders. The two mines had lifted the runners off their feet and shredded their bodies with spinning, ripping shrapnel. The cries of pain and horror did not last long. Darkness and eerie silence returned to the forest in short order. The smell of exploded ordnance and death settled into the cold night air.

Perry gathered his cousins and said, "Those are some nasty toys Ghost plays with. Let's go see if any of these new friends of ours are still breathing, and remember where the other mines are."

They fanned out and moved forward, using their night vision goggles to look through the carnage for survivors. Only one was hanging on to life. It was Isam. Perry raised his night vision goggles and knelt beside him, observing his smoking clothes and bloody face. He was breathing fast and shallow, trying to hang on to life as long as he could—fear and shock written all over his face.

"I told you not to run, Mr. Scumbag."

The man could barely speak, but he managed a weak smile and whispered a reply. "I … was never … good … at poker, Mr… . White Teeth."

Then, he was gone.

The cousins had gathered around by now, and Perry said a farewell to the dead invader.

"I doubt you will be seeing those beautiful virgins, Mr. Scumbag. Adios."

CHAPTER 30

Hostage Location
Melbourne, Florida

IN A CAREFULLY COORDINATED assault, the SWAT team simultaneously crashed through the front and rear doors of the hostage house and yelled POLICE! In a well-rehearsed maneuver, they poured through the entire house like an angry snake, yelling CLEAR as they confirmed each room was empty. All rooms were void of people except the living room. Quickly, the living room filled with heavily armed and body-armored policemen staring down at the forms of two men dressed in black, unconscious on the floor. Their handguns were still on the table in the middle of the room, and high-powered assault rifles were leaning in a corner near the door. It did not appear as if any of the weapons had been used, and there were no obvious signs of a struggle. There was an armchair sitting toward the back of the room with ropes still hanging from the arms and legs of the chair, but no sign of a hostage.

"What in the hell's going on here?" the hostage team leader wondered out loud. He reverted to his training and shouted instructions to the officers around him to search every room again, every cabinet and closet and appliance, the car in the driveway, the little tool shed out back, and look for signs of freshly dug earth in the yard. He called in the police chopper that was on standby and asked them to position themselves over the property and use their powerful searchlight to aid his men in their search. He put out an all-points bulletin to every law enforcement unit in the area to seal off any route leading in or out of the city and to be on the lookout for a hostage fitting Mrs. Flannery's description. Next, he asked the paramedic that always accompanied the SWAT team to examine the unconscious masked men on the floor and try to determine what had happened to them. He then called for the forensics team to double-time it down to the hostage scene and try to come up with a clue as to what might have happened to the missing hostage.

He stepped outside the house, took out his cell phone, and placed a call that he was not looking forward to making.

"Mr. Flannery, we have secured the house where we believe your wife had been held. The good news is that we have no reason to believe she has been harmed. The bad news is that she is not here, and the two men who we believe were guarding her are on the floor in an unconscious state."

"What? How can that be? That doesn't make any sense. Where could she be? And what happened to those guys who were watching her? Are there any signs of violence or anything like that?"

"No, Mr. Flannery, we did not observe any blood or signs of struggle or violence. We found a chair where it appeared, she might have been secured, but she is not here to our knowledge. I have my forensics people on the way down here to process the scene and hopefully provide some answers to all this. We are also in the process of doing an intensive search of the property and the surrounding area. We have a lot of work to do before we can come up with definitive answers."

"Oh God, I don't know whether to be relieved or terrified."

"Well, let's take the good news wherever we can find it for right now. I will keep you informed every step of the way and let you know the moment we come up with any new evidence or answers. Have you gone home yet?"

"No."

"It's going to be a long night and day while we work on this thing. I strongly suggest you go home and try to sleep a little. I promise to keep you in the loop. Just keep your phone on in case we have something to report."

"OK, you're probably right. I need to go home and take a nap and freshen up a little. Thank you, commander, for your quick action and for keeping me informed."

"It's what we do, Mr. Flannery. Talk to you soon."

Joseph pushed the End Call button on his cell phone and laid it down on the desk. He was numb. He was exhausted. He was scared. He had not eaten in hours, and the coffee he had been drinking had left him shaky and nervous. He missed Carol desperately and could not even let his mind entertain the thought that he might not see her alive again. He picked up the cell phone, put it in his pants pocket, gathered his suitcoat and briefcase, and made his way to the parking area outside his office. He hoped he could make the drive home without incident. He was losing his ability to focus at this point.

He dragged himself down to his government sedan, threw the suitcoat and briefcase onto the passenger seat, and fell into the driver's seat. He fumbled for the keys in his other pants pocket, dropped them on the floorboard, cursed under his breath, recovered them, put the house key in the ignition, pulled it out and put the right one in, and finally got the car started. He backed out, glad that nobody was in the space behind him, remembered to fasten his seatbelt only after the warning bell began dinging, and pointed the long sedan toward the front gate. He waved absentmindedly at the security guard as he passed through the gate and headed home. Joseph was running on autopilot by this time, and his subconscious took over the driving and delivered him safely to his house.

He pinched the garage door opener on the sun visor, pulled the big car into the spacious garage, and became painfully aware that his wife's SUV was not in its customary spot. He had come to take it for granted that she would always be home waiting for him. She always had.

The police had her car in impound and were searching it for clues to the identity of the kidnappers but had found nothing so far.

Joseph pulled his coat and briefcase out of the car along with his weary body, punched the button that closed the garage door behind him, and shuffled through the door that led to the kitchen area. He was hungry but decided he was much too tired to scrounge up anything to eat. As he walked towards the steps to his upstairs master bedroom, he allowed his briefcase to drop on the floor. He completed his climb up the stairs but hesitated before entering their bedroom. This had always been their special place, their sanctuary. Could he even sleep in their bed knowing she might still be in harm's way? Should he? With trepidation, he pushed on through the double doors of the bedroom, flipped the wall switch that turned on the lamp beside the bed, and threw his suit coat over a chair. As he somewhat reluctantly glanced at the bed, his legs grew wobbly, and he almost fainted. He grabbed the back of the chair to steady himself. He could not believe what his eyes were telling him.

Carol was lying on her back on their bed with a light blanket pulled up just under her neck. Her head was propped up on a pillow, her chest rising and falling slowly. Sleeping peacefully. Like an angel. *His angel.*

CHAPTER 31

Amir and his team froze in place as the two ominous explosions tore through the darkness. He pressed the talk button on his comm unit and tried to contact the Team Two Leader. No response. He tried again. Still no response. A bad feeling blossomed in his stomach, setting his teeth on edge. Had Isam's team used grenades? But those explosions sounded different than grenades. Where had he heard that exact type of explosion? Oh, no. He remembered now. Oh, how he remembered. *Mines.*

His blood ran cold at the thought of what might have happened to his brothers, and he urged his men forward at a quickened pace. Amir had to assume the worst at this point—that his other squad was no longer operational. He instructed his men to jog single file down the trail to minimize the risk of tripping a mine or booby trap. He fell back to the rear of the column.

Had their adversaries anticipated this attack? Or did his other squad wander into a booby trap?

Whatever the case, Amir knew that the element of surprise was no longer in play after those two explosions. They would have to strike fast and hard to have any chance of success. Maybe they would not anticipate the existence of a second force?

Through the trees, Amir could see the bright glow of outdoor floodlights coming from the perimeter of the house they were advancing toward. It was not that far away. They had not met any resistance yet. Perhaps, the enemy was still trying to organize and would not be ready for their attack. It was very possible they were concentrating on the area where the explosions came from and would not be expecting another intrusion from a different direction. Perhaps.

Suddenly, a brilliant white light assailed the assault team's eyes, blinding their night vision devices, and a voice commanded them to stop and lay their weapons down. Amir sensed there was no time to stop and see how this would play out. He had to push the situation to the limit and seize the initiative.

Amir yelled out a command in his native tongue, urging his men to open fire on the source of the light, and they responded by laying down a withering field of fire in that direction. The light was quickly destroyed, and they advanced only to discover there was nobody there other than what remained of a portable, handheld spotlight. The person who spoke had moved away from the light as soon as he finished. Another misdirection.

Amir remembered the warnings about his enemy's resourcefulness and became fearful they had been caught in another enemy trap. Were they being led up the trail or being goaded into stepping off into the woods?

Amir told his men to continue to advance up the trail as it was the shortest distance to the objective, and there was no way of knowing what lay in the woods. It occurred to him that Team Two may have run into the woods and encountered the mines there. Best to push forward and take the fight to the enemy.

Two shadowy figures now emerged from the trees alongside the trail where Amir's men were advancing. Screams pierced the night as the assault team was being engaged without gunfire. Amir squinted through his night vision goggles and could faintly make out the grisly scene taking place before him.

The two assailants were working with deadly efficiency to neutralize the four squad members in front of him. They had grabbed a man each and drew their knives across the men's throats before they could react. As the other team members were alerted by the gurgling screams of their dying comrades, the shadow men from the forest held their bleeding victims directly in front of them as a shield. While the remaining members of the assault team hesitated, not sure how to overcome this situation, or if their team members were still alive, the assailants moved quickly to take advantage of their hesitation. The two ghostly men drew their handguns and put a couple of rounds each in the heads of the two assault team members that had hesitated. Their heads were not protected by body armor. Just that quickly, the skirmish was decided. It took less than thirty seconds.

Amir watched in grim horror as his unit was neutralized. He took advantage of the situation to duck into the woods and continue to advance on the house. He would have to take his chances in the woods. Perhaps, he could still salvage a victory. Perhaps, they had left the house unguarded and deployed all their manpower to the trails. Perhaps, Allah would yet allow him to prevail over these infidel dogs. *Perhaps.*

Amir broke from the woods and into the clearing in front of the house. So far, so good. He could see through the windows into the dimly lit interior. The only person he observed was a small woman watching several video monitors.

Ha! He was right! They had left the house to be guarded by only a single female.

He advanced toward the front porch with his assault rifle pointed at the door, ready to take out the woman at the first sign of resistance, but he hoped to keep her alive long enough to learn where the treasure was hidden. He stepped up onto the porch, pulled open the screen door, twisted the doorknob to the heavy main door, and with a quick motion, he flung open the large door and burst into the living room.

Ha! The idiots left the front door unlocked!

The female looked up but did not react.

Amir raised his gun and threatened to shoot the woman if she picked up the pistol that lay next to her. He heard a rustle off to his left, and a man stepped from behind the open door and into his path.

Matt was holding his rifle by the barrel and leveled one of his powerful home run swings straight into the intruder's face. The shoulder stock of the weapon caught Amir flush on the nose and forehead. The unexpected blow knocked Amir off his feet and left him dazed and semi-conscious, sprawled out on the floor. Matt had taken it upon himself to guarantee that at least one of these murderous assholes would be taken alive, and this was the lucky guy that made himself available.

Matt flipped the gun around and pointed the business end toward the intruder's head. Matt could see that the man was clearly of Middle Eastern descent.

"Now you know why Americans love baseball, you bastard."

CHAPTER 32

The Flannery Residence
Titusville, Florida

THE COMMANDER OF THE hostage rescue unit stood in Joseph and Carol Flannery's bedroom, watching the paramedics work to bring Mrs. Flannery around. She appeared to be in a state of deep relaxation and sleep. She had not exhibited any signs of physical distress that they could observe. The medical team first tried smelling salts, but that only agitated her while she continued to sleep. They decided to inject Carol with a mild stimulant, and she was now coming back to full awareness. She blinked her eyes and struggled to shake off the drowsiness. She slowly sat up and looked around to see where she was. She saw the medical workers, the police, her husband, and realized she was in her own bed. She stared up at Joseph with a wide-eyed, puzzled look that said, *"How did I get here?"*

The commander looked at the paramedic, silently requesting permission to speak with the former hostage. The paramedic nodded in the affirmative and glanced at Joseph for his approval as well. Joseph, still stunned at this turn of events, nodded his head, indicating it was alright with him. The commander approached the bedside where Carol lay and gently took her hand.

"Hello, Mrs. Flannery. I am Dean Garrett, commander of the hostage rescue unit for this jurisdiction. We're glad to see you are unharmed. How are you feeling?"

Carol started to speak, but her throat was dry, and she rasped out a request for some water. Joseph always kept chilled water in a small refrigerator in their bedroom, and he quickly retrieved one and moved to his wife's side. He helped her sit up a little more and held the water bottle to her mouth while she took small sips. After her thirst was quenched and her throat was refreshed, she spoke in a hoarse whisper.

"Happy to see you, Mr. Garrett. Actually, I'm happy to see anybody. To answer your question, I'm feeling better by the minute. Just groggy, but fine other than that."

The paramedic interjected that all her vital signs were in the normal range and that other than some raw spots on her face, wrists, and ankles from being taped and bound, she seemed to be in good condition physically.

"Do you feel strong enough to answer some questions for us?" Commander Garrett asked.

"I think so," Carol replied, her voice gaining strength and clarity.

"Thank you, Mrs. Flannery—"

"If we're going to have a conversation, you're going to have to drop the Mrs. Flannery thing. I insist you call me Carol."

"Only if you agree to call me Dean."

"It's a deal."

"What do you remember, Carol?"

"Well, I remember getting pulled into a white van while I was opening my car door after shopping in Cocoa. They were parked next to me and grabbed me before I knew what was happening. I didn't even have time to scream for help before one of them put his hand over my face so tight I couldn't even breathe. They tied me up, put tape over my mouth, blindfolded me, and knocked me out with something by putting a cloth over my face. Once I woke up again, we were inside the house, and they had cut off the plastic ties that were around my wrists and ankles and had used ropes to tie me to an old armchair."

"Did they say anything to you that might give us a clue as to who they were or why they chose you?" Commander Garrett asked.

"Not at first. They didn't say much to me, and when they talked to each other, it was usually in Arabic or something."

"Not at first? Did they say something later that was important?"

"Just that it had to do with my son. But I think that was just a story they used to cover up the real reason. They probably thought they could get a fat ransom from the government if they kidnapped the wife of someone high up in NASA."

Joseph was listening intently and realized she was covering for Matt, just like he had.

"I see. Is there anything else of interest you can remember?"

"Yes, there is. You were in the house where I was held, right?"

"Yes, I was."

"Did you see that chair I was in with the bucket under it?"

"I did. What is important about that?"

"They made me go to the bathroom while I was still in that chair!" Carol was getting her voice and her spirit back now. "As I am sure you noticed, that chair had a hole cut out in the bottom, and I had to sit there and pee in front of them. They wouldn't even untie me while I did it. They pulled my pants down and watched me until I finished. I have never been so humiliated in all my life!"

"Did they do anything else to you … you know … like …?" Joseph asked, not at all sure if he wanted to hear the answer.

"No, they didn't do anything other than embarrass me. But they did insult me."

"In what way, Carol?" the commander asked.

"They said I was too old to be looked at in that way. I started to give them a piece of my mind about it, but they put the tape back on my mouth."

Everyone in the room stifled laughs at that remark.

"Can you tell me how you got free and made it home?"

"What do you mean? One of you brought me here … didn't you?"

Joseph spoke next. "No, we didn't, honey. I found you on the bed just as you are now when I came home about an hour ago."

"Wait … what? What are you talking about? Then who … how?"

"Take it easy, Carol. It's alright," Garrett said. "What's the last thing you remember?"

"The last thing I remember is sitting in that chair watching those two jackals play cards and make jokes that I couldn't understand. It was up into the night by that time, and I started getting real sleepy. Then, I guess I nodded off. When I woke up, I was here with you. I just assumed I had been found and rescued and brought home. But then, I would've woken up if that had happened. They must have drugged me."

"Well, the problem with that theory is when we broke into the house where we believed you were being held, the two guards were sound asleep on the floor, and you were nowhere to be found. We didn't know where you were until your husband called us and said he found you here."

"You've got to be kidding me. The guards were asleep?"

"Yes. They were in a deep sleep just like you. And, you have no recollection at all of anything that happened after you fell asleep in the chair and before waking up here?"

"No, Dean, I don't. This is really starting to get weird. So, you have those two guys in custody?"

"We do, and we had to wake them up just like we did with you. They were under pretty deep. I am going down to where we're holding them when I leave here, and I'll lead the interrogation. We need to find out who they work for and what their objective was."

"Yeah, I would like to hear those answers myself."

"I would too if I were you. I will keep you and Joseph aware of anything we find out. Good enough?"

"Good enough."

"Alright, you two get some rest, and I'll be in touch soon."

Joseph's mind had already moved forward to Matt's situation.

What's going on where Matt is? Is everyone okay? Should I tell Carol what I know or let her get some rest first? She has been through a lot.

CHAPTER 33

KELLI STOOD GUARD WITH her handgun while Matt used cable ties to bind Amir to a kitchen chair as the rest of the defenders gathered back at the cabin. No one was injured. The cabin defense was successful, and the threat neutralized for the moment.

"Ghost, I can't believe you let that sonofabitch slip past you," Jake said.

"Uh … I think he slipped by on your side, Jake."

"Like hell he did …"

Matt interrupted the good-natured ribbing between the old friends.

"Actually, I'm glad he *did* make it past you two. Otherwise, nobody would have survived. We needed to capture a live one this time. We've got to get some answers."

"Yeah, that was fast thinking, Matt. I think we should just arm you with a couple of baseball bats and forget the guns. You swing a pretty mean stick," Jake said.

Jake then turned to Perry and the cousins who were gathered near the door, watching the conversation.

"What happened out there, Perry?"

"We had 'em cornered on the trail just like we planned, and I warned 'em not to try to run into the woods. 'Course, we had 'em cut off so they could only run in one direction if they decided not to play nice. Then, after their leader and me had engaged in some stimulating conversation, he decided I was not telling him the truth about the woods being mined. So, he yelled out some kind of shit in another language, and they all broke for the trees. I don't guess I need to tell you the rest. You heard the results. Come morning, I don't think we'll find their bodies to be in very good shape. Just goes to show, you try to be nice to people …"

Amir had regained his wits and leered at Perry as he told the story. Hatred pouring out of his eyes. *If only I could get loose from this chair, I would kill them all and cut them up in little pieces and feed them to the dogs for what they did to my brothers.*

Matt observed the look of disgust on the captive's face, and it ignited a firestorm in his belly that instantly consumed him. The dam was breaking. He leaped forward and assumed a menacing position directly over Amir.

"You murdering sonofabitch! Don't you even look at us like we're the bad guys here. We didn't invite you bastards up here, and if you lost all your 'brothers,' that's on you, not us. In fact, if we hadn't been watching for you, you would have butchered every damn one of us, just like your brothers did to my friend Lucien. If I hadn't stepped out from behind that door when I did, you would've killed an innocent woman, you coward! Hell, I think I'll go ahead and kill you after all you low-life piece of shit!"

With that, Matt pulled his pistol, backhanded the man hard across the face with the barrel, then pushed the muzzle deep into Amir's forehead, forcing the man's head back and over at an unnatural angle. Matt's hand shook with an adrenalin-fueled rage, his finger twitching on the trigger, and he pulled the hammer back, preparing to fire. It appeared he had made up his mind to send the captive off to join his friends in Virgin Dreamland. Matt pushed the barrel even deeper into the man's flesh and began to squeeze the trigger. His neck was blood red, and sweat glistened on his face. He was nearing the point of no return.

Amir closed his eyes, preparing for the worst.

Jake yelled, "Don't do it!"

Kelli screamed, "Matt! Stop!"

Matt hesitated for a moment but continued to hold the gun right where it was. He looked over at Kelli, then Jake, revenge and fury shooting out of his eyes for all that had happened over the last few weeks. Everything he held dear had been threatened or destroyed. His wonderful life with Kelli, his friends' lives, his family's lives, his own life, even his boat and livelihood.

Somebody needs to pay and pay dearly, damn it!

He began to tighten his squeeze on the trigger again and was forcing the man's head even farther over backward.

"Matt!" Jake yelled again. "Hold up a moment. Listen, Pardner, I know how pissed off you are, and you have every right to be. We all are. And, if we didn't need to question this scumbag, I would be the first to tell you to waste his sorry ass. But this isn't who you are. You're better than this. You're the one that had the good sense to capture one of them alive. There will come a time for justice, I promise you. But that time isn't now. We need to find out who's causing all this hell in your life and go after them. It's the only way it will end. You know that. So, Matt, just ease that hammer back down and let me have some fun with our guest, okay?"

Matt considered Jake's words. Despite his raging emotions, he knew that Jake was right. But he was just so damned tired and angry. He held his position for a few more tense moments, then eased the muzzle away from the man's temple and took a step backward. Just as the captive thought the danger had passed and let out a deep sigh of relief, Matt stepped forward again and slammed a hard, straight right fist into Amir's already bloody face. The blow's impact sent Amir over backward, still bound to the chair. He groaned as his head bounced off the wooden floor, fresh blood flowing from his nose.

"He's all yours, Jake. Do whatever it takes, my friend. This needs to end here and now."

Jake thought, *C'mon, Matt. Don't cross over to the dark side. Once you do, you can never go back. I know.*

CHAPTER 34

JOSEPH PROPPED HIMSELF UP on one elbow and stared at his slumbering wife in the early morning light, the soft glimmer that steals through your window and chases the shadows. She looked so peaceful, so beautiful. Still youthful in both mind and body.

He suppressed a chuckle as he remembered her telling of being put off by the remark her captors had made about her being "too old." He was so lucky to have her as his partner in life. He was relieved and thankful beyond words to have her safely in their bed beside him again. What would he do if something happened to her? How would he function? She was the strength behind all he had accomplished. The steady and loving hand that kept their family ship on course while he fought the battles at NASA. He could not imagine his life without her in it. Nor did he want to.

He slid from under the covers and padded softly down the stairs and into the study. He dialed Matt's secure phone. The phone rang several times without an answer. Joseph's anxiety began to ramp up. Had something horrible happened there? Had he regained his wife only to have something tragic happen to his son? Fear's icy tendrils gripped his heart more tightly with each unanswered ring. Just as he was about to hang up and dial again, he heard Matt's voice on the other end.

"Hello."

"Matt, are you and Kelli alright? Are your friends alright?"

"Yeah, we're all fine, Dad. Listen, I'm sorry that I've not been able to get back to you. Things got a little complicated here."

"It's okay. I understand. I talked to Kelli earlier, and she told me what was going on up there. I knew you had your hands full. Did she give you my message?"

"She said you had called, and you couldn't wait any longer to call in the cavalry to help find Mom. Did the surveillance tapes show you where to look?"

"Yes, they did. Thank you for coming up with that idea."

"Have you found Mom? Is she safe?"

"Yes, she is here at the house with me right now."

"Oh, Thank God … I'm … uh …" Matt was having trouble talking through his emotions after hearing the news that his mother was safe.

"I felt the same way, son. Take your time."

"It's just … I couldn't have lived with myself if something would have happened to her on account of me and this crazy journey I'm on."

"I know … I know. But she's fine. She was unharmed and is resting comfortably. Now, tell me, how did things turn out on your end? Last I heard, Kelli said you were defending yourselves against an assault team?"

"That is accurate. As usual, Jake and Ghost had my back and kept us in one piece. I would have been dead several times over by now if it wasn't for those two. And we had some help from Ghost's cousins. They're some pretty bad hombres themselves."

"So, nobody got hurt?"

"I didn't exactly say that, Dad. I said all of *us* are okay. The bad guys didn't fare so well."

"How many were there?"

"We think there were ten in all."

"And, they're all dead?"

"All except one. I knocked him out before he got himself killed. Jake and Ghost are getting ready to interrogate him as we speak."

"I don't even know what to say about all this, Matt. Will you let me know what you find out?"

"I will. Did they catch the guys that kidnapped Mom, or did they have to take them down to save her?"

"Well, that's where it gets a little strange. You see, when the police stormed the house where she was being held, they found the two men who had been guarding her passed out on the floor. Your mother was not even there."

"You mean she slipped out somehow while they were sleeping?"

"No, it's stranger than that. The cops took the two sleeping kidnappers into custody, but there were no signs of Mom anywhere on the property and no indication of what had happened to her or where she had gone. They sent in all their investigators and were looking through everything and blocking the roads, trying everything to figure out where she was. So I came home while the authorities did their thing, and you won't believe this—when I came into the bedroom, your mother was fast asleep on the bed."

"Jesus, Dad! Seriously? How did she get away and make it to the house? And why didn't she call you?"

"Mystery of the century, Matt. The last thing your mom remembers is going to sleep while still tied to the chair in the house where she was being held. She said the guards were playing cards, and nothing unusual was going on. The next thing she knew, she woke up in bed with all of us staring at her. I had called in the hostage rescue commander and the paramedics. Your mother is as stumped as the rest of us. The paramedics had to give her a stimulant to wake her up, but other than that, she's in good physical condition."

"So, somebody drugged all of them, took her out of there, and put her in her own bed?"

"Not exactly. It gets even weirder. When the medical team ran drug screens on all their urine and did preliminary blood tests, they didn't find any trace of a knockout drug of any kind, or any other kind of drug for that matter."

"What did these two guards look like?"

"They were dressed in black and of Middle Eastern descent. Your mom said they talked to each other in Arabic, but they also spoke good English."

"Same MO for the bad guys here. All the men that came after us tonight match the description you just gave me. That's a good thing because it means they're all connected, and if we can get this guy to talk, maybe we can find out who's after me. But, there's a problem with that, too. The guys we encountered down in Florida and out on Bimini were totally different. They were from Eastern Europe. Russia and Ukraine, we think. So, I don't know if the two groups are connected or if I have a second group trying to get to me, too."

"Good Lord, Matt. Are you sure what you discovered is worth all this?"

"Yeah, I'm sure. And, someday, when I can share with you what I found, you'll be sure, too. Grandpa Bill was."

"Alright, Son. If you're that sure, it's good enough for me. And why, again, can you not share this information with me or the government or anyone else?"

"Because it compromises the safety of anyone who knows what it is."

"It seems to me that it's already compromising the safety of people who don't know what it is, so what's the difference?"

"Unfortunately, you're right about that. But, trust me, it would be worse than it is if you knew the rest of this story. And, I would be putting you in a position to make moral judgments and decisions about your future with NASA that you are better off not having to make."

"It sounds like your discovery has global implications."

"Actually, Dad, *it does*."

CHAPTER 35

THE CAPTIVE HAD BEEN roughly dragged, chair and all, to an outbuilding in the woods about twenty-five yards from the main house. It was a small windowless structure that seemed to have been built for situations just like this, though Ghost claimed it was intended to be a storage shed. Matt, Jake, and Ghost had taken turns pulling the chair and its occupant over the bumpy path through the thick woods, using flashlights to light the way. The nervous terrorist groaned and complained about his discomfort all the way there, but his petitions fell on deaf ears. They reached their destination and jostled the man and his chair into the middle of the building's single room. Ghost walked over to a table in the corner and lit a kerosene camping lantern. That was the only light in the room. It cast a dim pallor over the space, adding to the sense of foreboding that was building within Amir. Jake had taken a folding chair along and now set it directly in front of the man he was about to interrogate. He scooted the chair closer to the fearful man, sat down slowly for effect, and leaned in, nose to nose with his bound prey.

"What's your name?" Jake asked in an even, low tone.

No reply. The man just stared back in defiance, trying not to show fear in the face of the enemy, disregarding the likelihood of his impending death.

Allah be with me, he silently prayed.

It was daylight. Perry and the cousins had taken Ghost's four-wheelers into the woods to gather what was left of the night's attackers. It looked like a slaughterhouse in the woods where the mines had been tripped. They wrapped all nine of the remains in tarps and tied them securely. They hauled the bulging tarps back to the cabin for transport to another location. From there, they loaded the bodies into Eddie Johnson's long-bed, diesel, dually work truck and drove them to a deep gulley that sat at the bottom of a long ravine at the back of Eddie's property. Eddie ran an excavation business and would use his backhoe to dig a deep grave in which to hide the remains. Then he would cover the pit with dirt and a layer of heavy rocks that he had accumulated over many years of digging them out and hauling them off people's property. Kelli had remained at the cabin to do some cooking and baking. It was a needed distraction after that long, stressful night.

She did not want to know what was going on out there in that little building in the woods.

"I said … tell me your name," Jake repeated.

Sullen silence was the only response.

"I see you're not in a mood for polite conversation, so I will make up a name for you since you don't want to tell me the one your mother gave you. You did have a father and a mother, didn't you? Or were you a bastard?"

This was one of the worst insults that could be hurled at someone from Amir's part of the world. Jake knew that. He had operated in the Middle East on many occasions and understood the culture. Jake could see the man's eyes widen, and his body stiffen as the anger rose within him.

"Or perhaps … you're just a camel turd that stuck to the bottom of a nobleman's shoe, and it fell off in front of your mother's house, and she mistook you for a human and raised you?"

Jake was turning the screws hard now. Being likened to camel dung or hit with the bottom of a shoe were very serious insults in the Middle East. It implied you were lower than dirt … or dung.

"I will kill you! You miserable infidel!" The man could no longer contain his rage.

Jake sat back in his chair and smiled widely. "Hey, that's more like it! You can talk after all. Now, maybe we can have a friendly chat. This can go easy … or it can go hard. You choose. I'm comfortable doing it either way. Understand?" Jake was setting the ground rules and establishing control.

The man continued to shoot eye daggers at Jake, wishing he was a cobra snake who could strike with his head and shoot deadly venom into his interrogator's eyes.

Jake continued. "Okay, here's how it's going to work. I ask the questions, you answer them. If you answer them to my satisfaction, I give you my word you can leave when we're finished. We have no use for you. Just what you know."

The captive looked at Jake with disbelief. He did not believe he would be let go even if he talked. Therefore, he decided he would not speak to them. If they were going to kill him anyway, and he was sure they would, why give them what they want? Amir had no loyalty to the capitalist pig Dominion but did not want to assist this man who sat in front of him either. He would sell out Dominion in a minute if he thought he would truly be free to return to his homeland, but he did not see that as a possibility.

"So, here's your first opportunity to impress me, Mr. Camel Turd. Who do you work for?"

Silence.

"You're not impressing me, Mr. Turd. And here I thought we were going to get to know each other, have a pleasant conversation, and exchange addresses for this year's Christmas card list. Well, I am getting the feeling that you don't want to be friends after all."

With that, Jake nodded to Ghost, who reached into a large, black duffle bag that he had brought and produced a gleaming metal stick about two feet long and handed it to Jake.

"Do you know what this is, Mr. Turd?"

Amir did not reply, but apprehension flickered in his eyes as he surveyed the metal wand.

"It's a shame that you have chosen to be so unsociable, my friend. Do you not recognize this little gadget?"

Still no response from Amir, though his breathing was becoming quicker and more labored.

"I see from your reaction that perhaps you have seen it before. This is a magic nightstick. You may have seen these used back home in goat land or even used one yourself to have similar conversations with guests at your own parties?"

As Jake asked that final question, he thrust the stick forward into the groin of Amir and held it there for several seconds. A blood-curdling scream erupted from the depths of Amir's being. It reflected the anguish of having his privates subjected to a high voltage shock that spread from his groin and worked its way throughout his whole body. He almost passed out from the sudden assault on his nervous system. Amir's mournful wail carried through the woods to the main cabin, causing Kelli's hands to shake as she formed a pie crust and tried not to think about what was taking place a short distance away. She understood it had to happen, but that did not make it any easier to take.

Jake rested the cattle prod back on his shoulder and smiled affably at the man in the chair.

"Feeling more talkative now, Mr. Turd?" Jake asked.

"Why ... should I ... believe you will ... set me free?" The man gasped out the words through his heavy breathing.

"'Cause I said I would. I have no reason to lie to you. I *will* get the information I want from you even if it ends up costing you your life. So, refuse to cooperate and slowly be tortured to death or tell me what I need to know and walk out of here alive."

"I cannot believe you would ever set me free."

Jake looked over at Matt.

"Matt, would you be so kind as to lend me your shoe?"

The prisoner looked confused by the sudden change of direction.

Matt removed his hiking boot and handed it over to Jake.

"When you doubt my word, you insult me. You call me a liar. Therefore, I must insult you in return, or you will not respect me."

Jake stood up, bent slightly, and slapped the man hard in the face with the sole of the boot. Then he shifted the shoe to his other hand and raked the boot bottom across the man's other cheek.

"Now, do not insult me again, Mr. Turd."

Amir's brave façade was starting to show signs of wear. "Why do you continue to call me such names?"

"Because you chose not to tell me your real name so I could address you properly? That is not so much to ask, is it?"

"If I tell you my name, will you stop insulting me and addressing me as camel dung?"

"Of course. I prefer civil discourse. Now … your name?"

"My name is Amir."

"Amir what?"

"Amir Kabil."

Ghost pulled out his cellphone, typed in some characters, took a picture of Amir with his phone's camera, and sent out a text message.

"Very good, Amir Kabil. That wasn't so difficult now, was it?"

Amir just stared, not knowing what to expect next.

"Next question, Amir. Who do you work for? Who sent you?"

Amir feared that once he divulged that information, he would immediately be executed. He remained silent.

"Cat got your tongue again, Mr. Amir Camel Turd?"

"You said you would no longer address me in this manner?"

"Yes, but you have stopped cooperating again, Mr. Turd. That is in violation of our little agreement here."

"I fear you will kill me if I tell you more."

"Ah, I see. So, you are implying that I am a liar again? That I will not let you go if you cooperate even though I promised I would?"

"Ah … no … I did not say …" Amir mumbled, searching for a reply that would not worsen his already dire situation.

"Amir, I fear I have done you a disservice. I have asked something of you without providing you with the proper incentive and motivation to give it to me. Forgive me. I will correct this oversight right away."

Jake nodded at Ghost again. Ghost reached into the black bag and handed him a tool that resembled a large set of scissors. Jake held them up in front of Amir, clicking them open and shut several times for effect.

"Do you know what these are, Mr. Turd?"

Amir shook his head, tension building in his body and face, his eyes widening.

"They are called tin snips. They are used to cut through sheet metal. You can only imagine what they do to human flesh if someone is unfortunate enough to get 'snipped' by them. I think I will give you a little demonstration of just how effective this tool can be, Amir."

Jake leaned forward and used the scissors to begin cutting away Amir's pant leg, the snips cutting through the thick fabric as if it was hot butter. Amir's eyes looked as if they were going to pop out of their sockets, and his breathing became erratic and rapid. Jake worked his way slowly upward, purposely emphasizing each snip until he reached Amir's private area. Jake then cut away the cloth that covered his genitals.

"No! No! You cannot do that to me! I will no longer be a man. My wife will leave me. I will have no more children. I will be an outcast!" Amir shouted, panic invading his voice.

"Well … that *would* be rather bad, Amir, I agree. As an act of good faith towards our new relationship, I will start with something else."

Jake suddenly seized the index finger of Amir's bound right hand and snipped it off as easily as if it were a piece of paper. Blood sprayed, and screams filled the little building and surrounding woods. Jake let it bleed freely for a few moments and motioned for Ghost to step in. Ghost produced a first aid kit from his bag of tricks and wrapped a strip of gauze tightly around the stub to slow down the bleeding. Matt was a little nauseated by it all, but the resolve he had felt earlier still remained.

Whatever it takes. That's what he had said to Jake.

"Why did you cut my finger off?" Amir sputtered, his chest heaving, a mixture of sweat and blood rolling off his face. His eyes were as wild as a rabid wolf.

"That was your trigger finger, Mr. Turd, if I am not mistaken. I thought the world might be a safer place if you no longer had the temptation to use it."

By this time, the pain and stress were taking a deep toll on Amir. This torturer was clearly mad and would not hesitate to do anything to get what he wanted. Amir knew that if he did not tell the madman what he needed to know, he would suffer unimaginable pain before the angel of death came to give him sweet relief. If he did give up the information, at least death may come quickly.

Jake moved closer again and began snipping away at the last shreds of fabric hiding Amir's genitals. The blades were less than an inch away from neutering him. Amir felt the cold steel of the pinchers slowly closing around the top of his scrotum. He stiffened and screamed.

"Stop! Allah, help me! Just please stop. I will tell you whatever you want to know. Just promise me you won't take away my manhood. And, you must swear to me that when this is over, and you take my life, you will do it swiftly and be merciful in your last actions toward me."

Jake smiled, moved the large scissors away from the man's groin area, and laid them aside.

"Very good, Amir. I'm happy to see you have decided to do this the easy way. It was about to get a lot messier in here, and I hate cleaning up blood. Now … who sent you?"

"Dominion."

"Who?"

"Jordan Dominion."

"You mean the billionaire, Jordan Dominion?"

"Yes."

"What did he send you to do?"

"Find some ancient artifacts that you are hiding here and take them back to him."

"Is he the one who has been sending hit teams after us all this time?"

"Yes, it was him the whole time. He created the Brotherhood specifically for that purpose, but after the Brotherhood failed to get the artifacts, he hired my brothers and me to take over their mission. To get the job, I had to kill the former leader of the Brotherhood myself."

"I see. And, why would you want to do this job for Mr. Dominion?"

"For money. He promised us a great amount of money. But I wanted to steal the artifacts and sell them myself instead of turning them over to Dominion. I planned to use the money for jihad in my homeland as well as send money to the families of my men and me."

"Oh … so you were going to double-cross Dominion?"

"That was my plan."

"Wow, this is good stuff. Are there records of your phone conversations with Mr. Dominion on the cell phone we took out of your pocket?"

"Yes. I did not delete them as he instructed. I kept them as a bargaining chip in case I needed it later."

"Good thinking, Amir! As luck would have it, I just happen to have a cell phone camera handy. Would you mind giving us a statement of what you know about Mr. Dominion? After all, he's nothing to you, right?"

"I will cooperate as long as you honor my request."

"I'll do you one better. I'm still going to let you go free since you are so chatty now."

Amir stared again in disbelief.

Jake placed the cell phone in front of Amir and asked detailed questions about his relationship with Dominion and what he had done for him. The answers that came forth were damning. Amir gave Jake all he knew.

Satisfied he had gotten all the information that Amir could provide, Jake untied the captive from the chair while Ghost and Matt trained their weapons on him. Jake checked the bandage where the finger had been snipped off and tightened it to stem the bleeding further. Jake led Amir out of the building and toward the main driveway leading away from the cabin and to the highway. Matt and Ghost continued to follow close behind, weapons at the ready, to make sure Amir did not attempt any last-minute heroics.

Once they reached the main road, Jake looked at Amir and said, "I'm a man of my word. I told you I would release you, and now you're free to go. I'm sure you have a getaway car hidden somewhere nearby, so you're on your own. Happy Trails!"

Amir paused for a moment, still not believing he was going to be allowed to walk away. He was sure they would shoot him in the back as soon as he tried to leave, then decided he had nothing to lose. He broke into a run in the direction of the old barn where he had left the SUVs, occasionally looking back over his shoulder to make sure he was not being followed or shot at.

Can this be real? Am I really to live? To be set free? Allah, you have delivered me!

Amir continued to jog until he had left his torturers behind, and the gray tobacco barn came into sight. His pulse quickened as he approached the weathered structure. He ran around the backside of the barn and yanked open the squeaky sliding door with his good hand and began fumbling for the keys to the SUV he still held in his pocket. As his eyes adjusted to the dark interior of the barn, he could make out the two SUVs and something else. *Oh, no.* There was a large group of policemen there to greet him with weapons drawn and ready. He looked at their insignia, and it confirmed they were all Kentucky State Police troopers.

The lead officer addressed Amir.

"Mr. Kabil, we have a warrant for your arrest. It seems you have been very busy the last few years. You're on all the terrorist watch lists. Don't know how you managed to slip into this country undetected, but we have a lot of questions for you. Down on your knees! Hands behind your head!"

Amir dropped to his knees with a look of final resignation on his face and moved his hands above and behind his head. While he felt the handcuffs being clasped around his wrists, he noticed another group of men coming through the barn door. It was Jake, Ghost, and Matt.

"But you said you would set me free?" Amir pleaded.

"And I did," Jake responded.

"But these men were waiting for me."

"I said *I* would set you free. I didn't say anything about the police. When Ghost texted your name and picture to some of our friends in Washington, it set off alarm bells all over the place. They sent these gentlemen here to give you a ride to the fine government housing they have reserved for you. You must have done some pretty nasty stuff to be this popular."

"I fight the holy war, jihad. I have done nothing wrong."

"Well, maybe in the eyes of your version of God, you have done nothing wrong. But we infidels take a dim view of massacres of innocent women and children in public markets and all the other chickenshit stuff you do in the name of Allah. I have dealt with your kind for years, and I have seen what you do. You're cowards and murderers and rapists. That's all you are."

Jake looked at Amir one more time and spat on the ground in front of him.

"Alright, gentlemen. Get this piece of camel shit out of my face before I do something I shouldn't."

CHAPTER 36

Dominion Winter Estate
West Palm Beach, Florida

Jordan Dominion was taking his lunch on the patio that overlooked his Olympic-sized swimming pool and perfectly manicured grounds. The winter day was slightly overcast but warm and comfortable. It was an ideal setting, but he hardly noticed as he picked through his plate of tomato stuffed with chicken salad and fresh fruit on the side. He was distracted by other matters.

He had not heard a word from Amir and had not been able to raise him on the phone. The report should have been called in during the night. He needed to know if the relics had been secured, but he did not have a good feeling about the mission. *Another failure? Impossible.* His private jet remained on standby in Lexington, waiting to bring Amir and the artifacts back to Florida. *Why had he not reported in by now? I am sure we caught them by surprise this time and were successful. Is Amir trying to pull a fast one on me?*

Dominion looked up as his butler came through the large glass doors leading from the rear of the house to the pool area. He was flanked by two unfamiliar men in gray suits.

"I am sorry, Mr. Dominion. These gentlemen insisted on seeing you immediately, and I could not prevent them from doing so."

"Is that right? Who are you 'gentlemen' and why did you so rudely show up at my residence unannounced? And, how did you get past the front gate security?" Dominion asked.

The taller of the two men, standing to Dominion's right, replied, "Who *we* are is not important, Mr. Dominion. We have a federal warrant granting us the authority to take you into immediate custody. The security people at your front gate made the wise choice. They didn't want to be found guilty of obstructing justice. I doubt you pay them enough to make it worthwhile to go to jail."

The man who was speaking reached into his suit jacket pocket and produced a folded set of papers and held them open in front of Dominion's face, bending down and extending his arms so they could be viewed clearly.

"A federal warrant? What's this about?" Dominion asked in a surly voice.

"It is a federal warrant issued by a federal judge whose signature is on the back page of the document. If you read the part at the bottom of the front page that talks about just cause, it states that you are being charged with murder, attempted murder, kidnapping, conspiracy, sponsoring terrorism, aiding and abetting known terrorists, attempted piracy, money laundering, and the list continues on the second page."

"This is outrageous! What evidence do you have against me? I have done nothing, and you can't make any of these charges stick. I demand to call my lawyer before I go anywhere."

"That will not be permitted in this case, Mr. Dominion."

"What do you mean? I'm an American citizen. I still have my rights. I want to talk to my lawyer!"

The two men in gray suits approached Dominion, and one produced a set of handcuffs. "Please stand, sir. Do not resist."

"You can't just come into my house and handcuff me like a common criminal!"

"Actually, we can. And, as you can see from the warrant, we do not consider you to be a common criminal. You are quite an uncommon criminal from what we have determined. Now put your hands behind your back."

Dominion attempted to call their bluff one more time.

"You *do* know who I am, don't you? Your bosses have to be out of their minds to try a stunt like this. Hell, I probably put several of them in the positions they are in. Once I contact my lawyers, I'll be out of custody so fast it will make your head swim. And, anyone who has had anything to do with this trumped-up deal, including yourselves, will be in a lot of hot water. I promise you that!"

"Hands behind your back, Mr. Dominion. Don't make us embarrass you any further."

Dominion could see that his tirade had produced no effect, so he countered with a question. "When do I get to make my phone call?"

"You will not be making that call anytime soon, Mr. Dominion. We have a videotaped confession and telephone records of transactions between you and a terrorist named Amir Kabil. We also have videotaped confessions from two of Kabil's operatives who you hired to kidnap the wife of a high-ranking government employee. You are now classified as an international sponsor of terrorism. That, Mr. Dominion, is taken quite seriously in today's world. Therefore, you will be treated as such, including forfeiture of your right to legal process as a U. S. citizen. You will be subject to military-style tribunals and treated as any other terrorist. It's time to go."

"But wait. I want to say goodbye to my wife and children." He could see his wife's distressed face peering from an upstairs window.

"No time for that. You will not be allowed outside contact for the foreseeable future. Because of your actions, others have had to say goodbye to their loved ones permanently. We will be in touch with your wife and make her fully aware of the charges against you and what your status is going forward. We will also be questioning her to see if she was an accomplice to any of your actions."

"No, please leave her and the children out of this. I swear she knows nothing about any of my business dealings," Dominion pleaded.

"We will see Mr. Dominion. If what you say is true, she has nothing to fear. Now stand and put your hands behind you, please."

Dominion was in shock and disbelief. Amir had not only failed in his mission but had sold him out. He took a long last look at his estate and became aware of its beauty in a way he never had before. He thought to himself that the adage was true. You never fully appreciate something until you lose it.

The two government agents now moved to each side of Dominion, each taking an arm. They stood him up and cuffed his hands behind his back. They guided him through the house to a waiting black government SUV that was in the center of a three-vehicle caravan. The agents pushed him down into the back seat, forced him to the middle, took a seat on each side of him, and closed the doors. The caravan sped away from the mansion.

Dominion was still resisting the reality of it all. His endless greed and thirst for power had robbed him of his reason and, ultimately, his life.

The vehicles moved through the security gate of the compound, and Jordan Dominion's dreams of global domination came to a sudden and quiet end as the gates closed behind him for the last time.

Dominion exited the world stage with a whimper rather than a bang.

CHAPTER 37

IT WAS A CRISP morning in Appalachia that tickled and refreshed the senses. High, clear skies framed the hills in a backdrop of startling blue. The smell of wood smoke permeated the air. Most of the houses on the ridge used wood-burning fireplaces and stoves to supply much of their heat as the days grew colder. Money was always in short supply for those that called these hills home. Wood was plentiful and free. The residents used propane stoves and electric heaters as a backup when it got too cold for the wood burners to keep their simple homes comfortable.

Kelli rested in a rocking chair on the front porch of the log cabin that had been their safe haven over the last couple of days. Much had happened. Much she would like to forget. But they had survived and still possessed the storage crystals from Bimini Island. It all seemed so surreal.

Could these relics really be from Atlantis? What other secrets did the crystals contain? What would happen once the information got out into the world?

It was still too much to comprehend. She shook her head free of concerns and questions.

She had been the first to rise after a long and restorative night's sleep. They had all stayed awake during the day yesterday and finished the necessary clean up once Amir had been taken away. By dinner time, Kelli had served up a massive meal for not only the Four Musketeers but also for Perry and the cousins as well. They had certainly earned their keep. There were generous servings of country ham, mashed potatoes, cornbread (Ghost showed her an old family recipe made in an iron skillet), green beans, and corn. For dessert, Kelli had prepared an apple pie and a cherry pie. When it came time to do the dishes, everyone pitched in and pushed Kelli out of the kitchen to sit down and put her feet up. There had not been much to worry about in the way of leftovers.

Now, on this chilly but peaceful morning, as she kept a slow and gentle pace in her rocking chair, she decided there was a lot to be thankful for, even in the midst of all this chaos.

She continued to rock back and forth with her eyes closed, her hands wrapped loosely around a steaming cup of coffee, breathing in the aroma, and floating in the peace and quiet of an Appalachian sunrise. Only the voices of early rising birds broke the stillness. She remained that way until she heard someone in the kitchen rattling the coffee pot. She could tell it was Jake, always purposeful and slightly aggressive in his movements. He emerged from the house and saw her wrapped in a blanket, enjoying the crisp fall morning.

"Mind if I sit a spell, Miss Kelli? Or would you rather be alone?" Jake asked.

She peered up at his blue eyes that always had a conflicting mixture of humor and pain. A deep sadness lived in there, trying to stay out of sight behind his intense countenance. Her heart hurt for him sometimes.

"Not at all, Jake. Grab a rocker."

"You sure I'm not disturbing you?"

"Of course not, you silly man. It's a beautiful morning. You should enjoy it, too. I think you could use some peace and quiet."

Jake took the rocker next to Kelli. He sat for a little bit in silence, rocking in unison with her. He was avoiding eye contact with her. Kelli could sense that something was on his mind.

"What is it, Jake? I can tell when something is bothering you."

"It's hard to talk about. I … just … well, hell … you know."

Kelli smiled at Jake's awkwardness. He was fearless in battle and mush with a woman.

"Actually, I *don't* know. Out with it, Jake. We've been through way too much for you not to understand that you can talk to me about anything."

"Well … alright then. I'll give it a go. Here's the thing. I think the world of you and Matt. I think you know that. And I've had to do some things on this trip that I wish you hadn't seen. Things you won't be able to forget. It matters to me what you think, and I'm afraid you probably see me as a monster by now. I don't want to lose you as a friend. I don't have that many, so I can't afford to lose the ones I have."

Kelli was deeply moved that Jake was so concerned about what she thought of him. She thought about it for a few seconds, rocked a couple more times, then turned and looked Jake directly in the eyes. It took a moment, but he eventually lifted his eyes to meet hers.

"The truth is, that I wish I had not seen a lot of this stuff. It's been terrible and overwhelming at times. But the bigger truth is that had you not been with us and willing and able to do the hard things you did, none of us would be alive. I don't claim to understand how you do the things you do, but I thank God every single day that you jumped on that boat with us. I know what a good man you are inside. You never have to worry about that. Matt doesn't talk about it much, but I know he feels the same way I do. Probably more so. Everything you have done has been for unselfish reasons. The biggest worry I have about you … is you. Your state of mind and well-being. I'm concerned about the toll that all this fighting has taken on you over the years."

Jake rocked for a spell and considered Kelli's words. They each took a sip of their coffee and looked out at the sun climbing through the trees, winking down at them through the gently shifting evergreens.

"I appreciate your concern. I really do. Don't worry about me, though. I'm too old to undo all the things I've done. Not sure I would if I could. I think I made a difference when it's all said and done. Hard to say. But that was my intention. To make a difference. You're a good woman, Kelli. Matt's a lucky man. Not too hard on the eyes either. Any more like you at home?"

Jake had regained the twinkle in his eye and was steering the conversation back to a more comfortable and predictable place.

"No. No more like me back home. But I appreciate the compliment. If there was someone else back home, I would want her to end up with a good man like you."

Jake blushed, smiled a little, and looked down into his coffee. "Naw, I'd be the last person you'd want to saddle somebody with. I'm too set in my ways, and the crust on my hide has grown way too thick. Not sure I'm civilized enough for a normal woman to live with anymore."

"Maybe. But I'm going to keep my eyes peeled for a good woman just the same."

"Now Kelli, you start that matchmaking business with me, and you'll ruin a perfectly good friendship!"

They were both still laughing as Matt came through the screen door with his freshly poured mug of coffee, blinking the sleep out of his eyes.

"You all making jokes about me while I'm not out here to defend myself?" Matt asked.

"Hell, yes, we are!" Jake replied. "Pull up a rocker, Pardner, and sit a spell. We could all use a relaxing morning. You see Ghost, yet?"

"Yeah. He's in there stoking the fire and brewing another pot of coffee."

Ghost soon joined the trio on the front porch.

"Only one rocker left, old buddy. You better claim it," Jake said.

Ghost settled into the fourth rocker and breathed in the invigorating air. "Can you see why I love it up here?" Ghost asked.

"Yeah, I get it," Jake replied. "Men like us need some peace and quiet after what we've seen and done."

"It's a great place, Ghost, but I'm afraid I'll always be a beach and water kind of guy," Matt said.

"I'm with Matt on that one," said Kelli. "But I hope you will allow us to visit your getaway once in a while when this is all over? This would be my second choice if I couldn't be near the ocean."

"Of course, you're always welcome, my friends. Hospitality is a tradition in these parts. I'm afraid I've not been as good a host as I normally would, but it *has* been a little hectic since we got here," Ghost said with a grin.

They all sat in silence for a while, sipping their coffee and creaking back and forth, lost in their own thoughts, enjoying the peace and quiet and each other's company. They had been through a lot together and had developed a deep bond with one another. Ghost went inside and brought the freshly brewed pot of coffee out with him. He topped off everyone's mugs, set the pot on a porch table, and returned to his rocker.

"What now?" Jake asked, looking at Matt.

"Well, with Dominion and his crew off our backs, I guess we should head back home and try to figure it out from there. I've got to talk to the insurance company about my boat and check on the house," Matt replied.

"Yeah, I've got to get back to the marina and make sure my employees haven't stolen me blind or put me out of business by now," Jake added.

"I've got to go back to my dive business. I'm afraid I'm going to lose all my students if I don't show up soon," Kelli said.

"If it's all right with you, folks, I'm going to stay here and rest my bones for a while," Ghost said.

"I don't blame you, Ghost. You've certainly earned it," Matt said. "I'll never be able to repay you for what you've done."

"Nothing to repay. A friend called. I came. End of story. Now I have new friends."

Matt just shook his head. *Where do people like this come from?*

"So, Jake, I'm a little nervous about traveling with these artifacts," Matt said. "I'm still paranoid from being chased for several weeks. What do you think would be the best way to get them home?"

"Well, Compadre, that's a very good question. As far as flying, we don't want to check the relics through security in a piece of luggage, and I don't know what effect an x-ray machine would have on those crystals. I don't think we can even try to put them into a carry-on bag and sneak them through regular airport scanners. I'm pretty sure those artifacts would light up those scanners like Fourth of July fireworks. And then, we would be in a world of trouble again. So, we need to either drive back or pay for a private flight that doesn't force us through airport security."

"You're right, as usual, Jake. Have you heard any more from your friends at the CIA?"

"Nope. Nothing yet."

"But, you will eventually … right?"

"Pretty sure they'll want to ask some questions before it's all over. I wish I could tell you different, but I'd be fibbing."

"Well, if it's alright with you and Kelli, I think we should just have Ghost take us to a rental car agency, rent a car, and drive back. It would be a lot less expensive, and if we take turns driving, we can be there in about fourteen hours. We won't have to take a chance with any airport security, either."

"Probably the safest way to transport these things right now," Jake said.

"That's fine with me," Kelli said. "When do we leave?"

"Early tomorrow morning okay with everyone?" Matt asked.

Kelli and Jake nodded in agreement.

"I'll take you guys down to Morehead this afternoon and pick up the rental car if you want," Ghost offered. "It's the closest town that would have a large rental agency."

"Thanks, Ghost. That would be great. Then we can have the car loaded and ready to get an early start," Matt replied.

After lunch, they all loaded into Ghost's Jeep and made the trip into Morehead, where they rented a white GMC Denali SUV. It was big and offered a lot of room for them to stretch out during the long trip. It also featured an abundance of cargo space to stow their bags. It was already full of fuel, and they made their way back to Ghost's cabin on Johnson's Ridge. Ghost stopped on the way and picked up a few more items for supper.

Once back at the cabin, Ghost insisted on having another cookout. He barbequed chicken breasts and grilled fresh ears of corn still in the husk. The late fall harvest was still supplying the local grocers with fresh corn. Kelli baked scalloped potatoes and brownies, and the feast was on. They shared the good wine Ghost had been saving for a special occasion and ate their fill. The Four Musketeers retired to the sitting area around the stone fireplace and finished off the evening with lots of wine and laughter. It felt good to finally savor each other's company without fearing for their lives. To be able to watch the fire dance and listen to the crackle and pop and not think it was the sound of a firearm being discharged. They had been informed by the state police that Dominion was already in custody and being charged as a terrorist. The state police had been advised by higher authorities not to push an investigation into the attack on Ghost's cabin. They had been briefed on the background of Jake and Ghost and that the matter would be handled by the Feds going forward.

The four friends retired to their beds early and enjoyed the best night's sleep they had gotten for many long days. The morning came fast, and they were up before dawn, showering and doing their last-minute packing. Ghost was already in the kitchen, brewing the coffee and making bacon and egg biscuits for them to eat before heading out on the road. He also prepared a thermos of coffee for them to take with them.

The remaining Three Musketeers wolfed down their breakfast biscuits and a first cup of coffee. They got some go cups out of the cabinet and made coffee for the road. They grabbed the thermos and the last of their bags and went outside to load the Denali. Soon, everything was in its place, and Matt volunteered to drive the first leg of the trip.

Matt and Jake both gave Ghost long bear hugs and thanked him again for all his help and hospitality. Kelli then stepped forward and attempted to get through her hug with dry eyes, but it was a lost cause. She threw her arms around Ghost's neck and held on for a long time, wetting his shoulder with tears of sadness and gratitude. Finally, she stepped back and made a beeline for the back seat of the car so she could compose herself. Matt climbed into the driver's seat, and Jake took shotgun.

With a final wave goodbye, they wound their way off the mountain to whatever awaited them at home.

Nothing would come easy.

CHAPTER 38

Matt's Bungalow
Anna Maria Island, Florida

THE ROAD TRIP BACK to Florida was uneventful. No surprises. No ambushes. Lots of naps and sandwiches. Good conversations. No conversations. Everyone had a lot to process. They drove straight through taking turns at the wheel, only stopping for gas and food and arrived at Anna Maria Island just after midnight. Matt dropped Jake at his house and headed to the beach bungalow.

"You think maybe I should go home tonight and see if my place is still in one piece?" Kelli asked in a tired voice.

"No chance. I can't imagine not having you beside me tonight. You've become habit-forming," Matt replied.

The response caught Kelli a little off guard. It surprised her, in a good way. She could not suppress a smile. She was relieved to hear that Matt felt that way after all they had been through. She certainly felt closer to Matt than ever before and had been curious as to how this whole thing had affected his feelings toward her.

This trip had confirmed to her that he was truly the man she had always believed him to be. She did not want to be by herself tonight. She felt a little apprehensive about being alone. It was hard to shake the feeling that someone was always after them.

They pulled into the sandy parking spot at Matt's home, unloaded their bags, and half-dragged everything into the house. Their weariness was a constant companion now it seemed. Matt left the bags of clothes at the bottom of the stairs and shuffled into the kitchen for a drink of water before bed. He switched on the light and was reminded of what started all this. The bloodstain on the wall from his battle with the intruder persisted. It would take another coat of primer and paint to make it go away. The stain on his memory never would.

Kelli came into the kitchen behind Matt and noticed him staring at the discolored spot on the wall.

"You okay?" she asked.

"Yeah. I just can't believe all the crazy stuff that's happened. It seems ages ago that all this started right here in this spot. It doesn't seem real to me at times. It was just a short time ago that we were drinking margaritas with Lucien right here in this kitchen. I miss him."

"Me, too," Kelli replied. "What do you say we get our water and head up to the love nest? We haven't spent a night there in a long time, and I think I hear it calling us. We can talk this through tomorrow when we are a little more rested."

Matt looked at her, and an impish grin crossed his face. "Race you upstairs!"

CHAPTER 39

Jake's Marina
Anna Maria Island, Florida

JAKE WAS CLOSING THE marina office at the end of his first day back on the job. Other than taking care of some matters that had been deferred until his return and having to soothe a couple customers' ruffled feathers, Jake did not have as many things to catch up on as he had expected. His employees had handled things well in his absence. It had been a good test of their loyalty and capabilities. Or maybe they were just afraid to cross him. Either way, he would worry less about things next time he needed to take some time off.

He was saying his goodbyes to the workers as they made their way out when he saw a black sedan pull up in front of the office. He knew who typically drove that kind of car, and he braced himself.

Shit. Here it comes. Payment is due.

Two men in dark suits and sunglasses got out of the front of the car and headed to the office door. As they entered, they took off their sunglasses and looked at Jake. The one on the left broke out into a big grin.

"Jake, you crusty old bastard, how the hell are you?" the man said.

Jake returned the grin and walked from behind the counter to shake his hand.

"Better than you, I'd bet," Jake replied. "Jesus, John, you got nothing better to do than go around pestering your old crew?"

"Actually, I don't. Since they assigned me to an office and a desk and made me a supervisor, I don't get to come out in the field and create havoc like I used to. By the way, this is my assistant, Special Agent Avery Thompson."

Avery stepped forward, shook hands with Jake, and they exchanged short pleasantries. Jake quickly assessed him to be a newbie and not to be trusted. Those types were always looking to make a name for themselves and usually at someone else's expense. The new ones thought they had all the answers, but the reality was they routinely screwed things up for the veteran operatives in the field.

"Avery has much the same background as you, Jake. But, not as much experience, of course. He's a Yale graduate and the powers that be, decided he should come inside and learn to run a team. He is fully aware of who you are and your Agency résumé."

"How nice. It's always good to see you, John, but I don't suspect you two came all the way from Virginia just to have a beer with me?"

"Well, we can have a beer if you want, but no, I need to ask you some questions."

"And, the 'powers that be' decided since you were my handler for all those years, that you would be the right guy to do the askin'?"

"Pretty much sums it up."

"I can't say I'm surprised. I figured one of those black government sedans would be showing up before long. You guys should really consider something less obvious. Hell, nobody drives those cars anymore except government people. It looks like something out of a *Men in Black* movie."

John Milburn chuckled at Jake's observation. "You know, old friend, I couldn't agree more. I think we should switch to silver Bentleys. So, where do you suggest we go so we can talk?"

"How 'bout we take a ride down to the Bridgetender Inn? We can get a table down by the water and have something to drink and a bite to eat while we have our little talk."

"Sounds good to me. You okay to ride with us?" John asked.

"I don't know. I'm a respected businessman on this island, and being seen with you guys could besmirch my spotless reputation," Jake replied with a straight face.

"Same ol' Jake. It's good to know that some things never change. Alright then, you drive, and we will follow in the *Men in Black* car."

"Fair enough. Mind if I wash some of this grease off my hands before we go?"

"Of course not. Take your time. We'll be out in the car."

Jake walked back into his shop and into the employee restroom. He pulled his cell phone out of its holster and typed a short message: Old friends here to talk. Headed to Bridgetender. I'll do what I can.

He sent the text to Matt's cell phone, deleted the message from his own, washed his hands, and returned to the front lobby, locked the front door, and headed to the parking lot where his visitors awaited.

Jake leaned down and spoke through the open driver's window of the sedan, "Alright guys, time for a cold one, and you might want to lose those ties and jackets. You *are* on an island, you know, and you'll attract more attention than a naked woman on the beach."

CHAPTER 40

Matt's Bungalow
Anna Maria Island, Florida

MATT AND KELLI HAD managed an intimate interlude, spooned, passed out, slept hard, and rose early. There was a lot to catch up on. They spent the day checking e-mail, making phone calls related to their businesses, chatting with friends and family to let them know they were home and were now relaxing in deck chairs on the lanai facing the restless Gulf of Mexico. And, of course, they were sipping perfect gold margaritas from their favorite glasses.

Matt's cell phone buzzed on the table next to his drink. He looked over at the phone, noticed Jimmy Buffett still smiling at him from the side of his drink glass, then picked up the phone and read the text message.

"Well, it looks like the chickens are coming home to roost, as my grandfather used to say."

"What do you mean? Who's that message from?"

"It's from Jake. His buddies from the CIA are there with him right now to ask some questions. He took them up to the Bridgetender to talk. He said he would do what he could, but this is a very tricky situation for him. He'll have to be careful about lying to them while still trying to protect me. As an ex-operative, he could get sent to prison for not being truthful with them. Especially after calling them for assistance to get us home."

"Oh God, Matt. It seems this trouble will never end. What should we do?"

"Well, I knew this would happen pretty soon. To be honest with you, I don't know what to do. I can't just stay on the run. I don't have the money or the stomach for it. I ran up some pretty high credit card balances while we were gone and haven't made any money in a while. I have a little savings, but it wouldn't get me far. It wouldn't take them long to catch up with me anyway. I've been thinking about this, and I think it would be best if you took the artifacts and went to stay with Isobel on Bird Key for a few days, at least until this cools down a little. That way, they can't question you right away, and if they search my house, they won't find the artifacts. That might buy us some time while I see what happens with the CIA and Jake."

"I really don't want to leave you in this situation, Matt. But as much as I hate to say so, it's probably the smart thing to do. When do you want me to leave?"

Matt smiled, looked lovingly at Kelli, reached over and gripped her small hand, and said, "Let's get one thing straight. I don't ever want you to leave. But, under the circumstances, it might be best if you call Isobel and head over there first thing in the morning. I don't think they will bother me before tomorrow. They will need a little time to digest the info they get from Jake before they make their next move. And, it will give us a chance to finish these margaritas and retire early … if you know what I mean. We need to make up for lost time."

Kelli looked at Matt with her wide green eyes, raised her drink glass slowly to her lips, took her time licking off some of the salt around the rim, and replied in a low, seductive tone. "Why Matt Flannery … that's the best idea I've heard in days. Never been intimate with an outlaw before and I find that idea to be … rather stimulating. Hope you got plenty of rest last night, mister. You're going to need it."

CHAPTER 41

"So, Jake, I hear you went on a little adventure recently?" John Milburn said as he turned his half-empty beer bottle around in circles with his fingers. He was staring at the bottle and avoiding direct eye contact with Jake. It was an uncomfortable situation these fellow warriors found themselves in.

Jake ignored the question for the moment and looked around at the tropical surroundings. Sarasota Bay in front of him, the blanched, crushed shells under his feet, the pastel-colored chairs on which they sat, the magical, golden light of another sunset, boats floating at anchor, the pretty girl at the bar holding court, and the ice-cold beer in his hand. He had settled in this little corner of paradise in a quest to find peace of mind. But, in the back of his mind, he always knew that once you worked for the Shop, you are never truly free.

Jake now turned his attention to John Milburn, the man who had served as his handler through more dangerous days and perilous missions than he cared to remember. They had always been on the same side and seamless in their pursuit of a single purpose. They shared a depth of friendship and familiarity that few ever achieved with another human being. That kind of bond is forged by trusting someone with your life and general welfare on a continuous basis. In spite of all they had shared, Jake now found himself on the other side of the table from John … literally and figuratively. Jake had requested and used CIA resources and assets, and the time had come to pay the piper with the information his old employers required. Jake understood their friendship would allow him some leeway, but only so much. John still actively served in the black ops section of the CIA and had to carry out his orders like the good soldier he had always been. Jake understood that. He, too, had been a servant to that master for many years.

"So, how do you like this place, John? Did you get plenty to eat and drink?" Jake stalled.

John looked at Avery, smiled knowingly, and turned back to Jake.

"It's a great place, Jake, and we've had all we want to eat. Not sure about the drinks yet. The night is young, and under different circumstances, you and I would show my young associate here how real men party. But for now, we need to get down to business."

"Alright, if you insist on messing up a perfectly good evening. What kind of burr does Uncle Sam have up his ass?" Jake asked.

"I need to know some details about that little trip you just got back from," John said.

"It was a nice vacation. Been working seven days a week since I bought that marina and needed a break. Went to Key West and the Bahamas on a friend's boat."

John was starting to screw his face into a frown now. "C'mon, Jake. Let's not play games. You and I are way past that. You and your friends got into a shit storm down there, and we had to come get you. That's not a typical vacation. Not even for you. Now tell me what really happened and how you got involved."

"Okay. You already know who I was with. I know you have the Coast Guard reports, the Navy file, and God knows what else at this point. It started out as no big deal. My friend Matt, who keeps his boat at my marina, had somebody try to kill him in his own house. When he decided to go on this trip to look for answers, I was worried his life might still be in danger, so I volunteered to go with him and watch his back. He had no idea what my background was. From there, things sort of escalated, you might say."

"Escalated? Jesus, Jake! There was a war going on out there on the water. And, I probably don't know the half of it. How many bodies did you haul into Coast Guard Station Key West? Then that engagement between Biscayne and Bimini? Took a couple of Hellfires to pull your ass out of that mess! Next thing I know, I hear you have Ghost with you. You two shouldn't be running any operations together without our knowledge and sanction. You know that. Were there other incidents or casualties I don't know about yet?"

"Well … yes … but only a couple. Whoever these guys were, they were well funded and damned if they didn't just keep coming. I had no choice but to defend myself and my friends. You would have done the same thing in my shoes."

John stared at Jake for a few moments to consider his story, then continued in a softer, lower tone. "I know you suffered a casualty while on Bimini. I was sorry to hear that. We did return the remains to his family as you asked, and they were grateful. And we created a strong cover story for his passing."

"Thanks, John. We all appreciated you doing that. His name was Lucien. He was a decent guy that got caught in a tough situation. We came up against some bad hombres."

"What were these guys after that was so damned important, Jake?"

"They worked for some rich guy who thought we had some treasure maps or something."

"Jordan Dominion," Avery Thompson injected.

Jake shot a withering look Avery's way. He did not feel obligated to answer questions from this Ivy League rookie.

John quickly noticed the death glare Jake aimed at his partner. "You might want to let me handle the questions, Avery," John interceded.

Avery's mouth drew into a tight, straight line, his face flushed slightly, and he looked out towards the bay. He decided to take a long drink of his beer to drown his frustration over the rebuke.

"Yeah, Dominion," Jake said.

"So … *did* you have treasure maps or something?" John asked.

"Well, sort of but not really. Matt Flannery's grandfather was a big history guy at the University of Florida, and he had done a lot of exploring around Bimini. He left some clues and stuff for Matt to follow up on someday, but it didn't seem like a big deal until somebody tried to murder Matt in his kitchen."

"So, you're trying to tell me this is just a big misunderstanding, and Dominion had operatives chasing you all over the place, sustaining multiple casualties and expending valuable resources, just for some worthless maps and trinkets?"

Jake looked John directly in the eyes. The moment of truth had arrived. If he did not tell at least some of the real story, the CIA would find out anyway and could strip him of all his government pay and benefits and even charge him and his friends with multiple felonies.

The dance floor was getting real crowded, and Jake was having trouble finding a safe place to two-step.

"I didn't say that … exactly," Jake replied.

"Then, damn it, Jake, what exactly *are* you saying?"

"Look, John, Matt is my friend and the most decent man you will ever meet. He needs some time to sort all this out and come to terms with everything. Do we need to do this right now?"

"I'm afraid we do. Good guy or not, we need to know what we got pulled into on North Bimini. Directors way above my pay grade are asking me questions and want answers. Hell, we even have jurisdictional issues to deal with on your behalf. We have attempted piracy and a gun battle to explain to the authorities in Collier County, Florida, where you had your first engagement at Ten Thousand Islands. The commander at Coast Guard Station Key West has lobbied on Matt's behalf, but still faces questions about the bodies he inherited. Then, you picked up Ghost and went to Key Biscayne, and something happened there. We're not sure what, and the Dade and Broward County sheriff's offices are investigating as well as Coast Guard Stations Miami and Homestead. Then you go out into international waters and have a full-blown combat engagement involving the U. S. Navy and one of their Predators. Next, you take a damaged ship into North Bimini, end up in a pissing match there—in a foreign country no less—sustain a casualty, and call me to bail you out. And you don't think I need to come up with some answers? You've got to help me on this one, or I might not be able to cover for you."

"Well, hell, John, when you put it that way, it sounds pretty bad, don't it?" Jake grinned broadly at his former handler.

John looked at Jake, slack-jawed at his comment. He tried to maintain a poker face, but he could not help himself. He burst out laughing at Jake's typical response to overwhelming odds. Avery did not get the joke, of course.

"God, Jake. If that doesn't take me back. How many times have I heard you make a wisecrack like that in the middle of a hopeless situation? Somehow, we always got you out alive, or *you* got you out alive. Alright, I'll tell you what. I'll do you a favor for old times' sake. You've got twenty-four hours to get your friend ready to talk about all this, and I'm holding you accountable for keeping him here. No running. That would really bring the heat down on everyone. I've got to have some answers that make sense. Something I can sell to my higher-ups. Fair enough?"

Jake raised his beer bottle to John, and they clinked bottles. "For old times' sake."

CHAPTER 42

Isobel's Estate
Bird Key, Florida

KELLI LEANED OUT THE driver's window of her pickup truck and punched in the code that opened the security gate to Isobel Renner's Bird Key estate. Isobel was Kelli's paternal grandmother, but Kelli never called her "grand" anything. Isobel would not hear of it. She insisted on being addressed as Isobel. The sprawling Bird Key estate had been home to Kelli for several years of her life. After her parents battled through a contentious divorce while she was in her early teens, Kelli asked permission to come live with Isobel, whom she dearly loved. Isobel took her in without reservation and became her surrogate parent. Kelli's biological parents were relieved to know they would not have to deal with joint custody of a teenage girl, and Isobel was delighted to have Kelli living in the big house with her. Isobel had been widowed years earlier, and the large home that overlooked Sarasota Bay had become too empty and too quiet. Kelli had been spending more and more time there anyway, so it was not much of a change for anyone. Even though Kelli had since graduated from the University of Miami's marine biology program, established a dive business, and created a great life on her own, this still felt like home to her. A safe space that was always available when she needed it most. Even in a moment like this. Especially in a moment like this.

Kelli swung her truck around the half-circle driveway in front of the main entrance, put it in park, turned off the engine, and hopped out to find Isobel. She did not have to go far. Isobel was watching through the front door and joyfully stepped out under the wide entry portico to greet her. They shared a warm hug, and Isobel accompanied Kelli back to the truck to assist in retrieving her bags, then carried them into the house and upstairs into Kelli's old room. The room was just the way Kelli had last seen it. Isobel always kept it the same and made ready for her visits.

"Just leave the bags for now Kelli, and let's go downstairs, and get something cold to drink, and sit out by the pool. I want you to tell me everything that's happened since you've been gone."

"I know it's still morning, but you better fix something strong if you want to hear these stories," Kelli said.

"That I can do, my dear girl. I just happen to have some fresh rum runners chilling in the refrigerator. Will that work?"

"That would be perfect."

Once downstairs, Isobel went for the rum runners, and Kelli grabbed a couple of her favorite drink glasses from the bar cabinet. The glasses were clear with short stems on the bottom and island scenes hand-painted on the sides. Kelli always felt so "tropical" when she drank from those glasses. It was like a vacation in a glass.

They poured the drinks, walked out the back of the house to the pool area, arranged the chaise lounges alongside one another with a small table between them to set their drinks on, donned their sunglasses, and settled in for a long talk.

They took a couple of long sips from their drinks, reveling in the taste of the fruity rums mixed with the bright morning sunshine and the friendly breeze wafting in off the Gulf. It was the beginning of the winter season in South Florida, and the humidity was no longer so oppressive.

Isobel opened the conversation. "Are you okay, Kelli? You look rather tired and stressed, dear."

"I'm fine."

"I'm not sure what 'fine' means, my little vagabond, but I've known you since you were born, and I can tell when you are stretched a little thin."

Kelli looked down at the pool water, clear and placid, like liquid glass. The pool pump had not kicked on yet, and it was a perfect setting on a beautiful morning.

Isobel's estate sat on a point of land at the end of the little peninsula known as Bird Key. Sarasota Bay opened out directly in front of them, the Gulf could be seen just beyond the Bay, and the burgeoning skyline of Sarasota bustled slightly out of view to the east. An egret soared high above their heads, searching for breakfast. A pelican, with its large bill tucked into gray and white wing feathers, was napping on a dock piling at the water's edge. A couple of boaters were idling out of the no-wake zone toward open water, waiting to open up their throttles and feel the warm wind on their faces.

Kelli felt at peace. So far removed from the events of the last couple of weeks. *Did it all really happen, or was it just a bad dream?* She thought about the storage crystals that were hiding in her bag in the bedroom upstairs. No, it was all too real. She pushed back to reality and her grandmother's close scrutiny.

"You're right. I know I can't fool you, and I don't really want to. I just hate to worry you. But I could sure use someone to talk to after all that's happened. It has been unbelievable. I'm not even sure where to begin."

"I know you were with Matt on the boat when you left. Is he alright?"

"Yes, he's fine. He is truly a wonderful man and one of my two best friends, counting you," Kelli replied with a smile. "But we're lucky to be alive, and this tale has a lot of arms and legs. The scariest thing is, it's far from over."

"Well, the best place to start is at the beginning. So, take a big drink of your cocktail, and let's hear it. We've got all day, my dear. Just us two birds here on Bird Key."

CHAPTER 43

Matt's Bungalow
Anna Maria Island, Florida

MATT'S CELL PHONE RANG, and he saw Jake's name pop up on the screen.

"Hey, Jake. Get any rest last night?"

"Not much. You and I have to talk, Compadre, and soon."

"Got to do with your visitors last night?"

"It does, and I could only hold them off for twenty-four hours. This time they want to talk to you, and I can't stop them."

"It's okay, Jake. I get it. I appreciate you trying to buy time for me, but I have to deal with this now, somehow. It's not going to go away, and I can't run from the CIA."

"You could, but I wouldn't recommend it. Right now, they're being pretty friendly and are mainly curious. But they want answers. They already know something real interesting is going on. They have Dominion in custody, and he's probably spilling his guts and trying to cut a deal with them. So, I would guess my old friends are quite intrigued at what they're hearing and want to know what your side of the story is."

"I understand. Can you come over here?"

"I can. How 'bout I grab us some sandwiches for lunch on the way?"

"That'll work. Thanks, Jake."

"No problem. See you in a couple of hours, Pardner."

CHAPTER 44

KELLI RETOLD THE EVENTS of the last couple of weeks while she worked her way through a couple of rum runners as well. She explained about the attempt on Matt's life that started it all, the appearance of Lucien in their lives, the attack south of Marco Island, Jake's heroic actions, Coast Guard Station Key West, the terrible night at Key Biscayne and No Name Harbor, the horrifying attack west of Bimini and how they were saved by a drone, her desperate dive to save the artifacts, their arrival at North Bimini, the expedition to Cayce Point and losing Lucien there, the escape to Kentucky, and surviving another assault at Ghost's cabin. Now they were safely home, but the CIA was coming for answers.

Isobel listened intently as the astounding tale unfolded. She remained quiet and asked no questions, only arching an eyebrow and blinking in surprise from time to time. Now, Kelli became still, emotionally and mentally spent after recounting the harrowing events they had endured, having to relive them in the telling.

"That's quite a story. Thank you for trusting me with it. I know you have held this information very close. Where are the artifacts, if I may ask?"

"They're upstairs in my bag. Matt knew the CIA would be visiting him soon, and he didn't want the artifacts in his house where they could confiscate them. I hope that's okay."

"Of course, it is. It will take them a while to gain access to this place, even if they decide to search here. And, I have some excellent hiding places we can use if it comes to that. What do you expect to happen next, dear?"

"Well, Jake has already been questioned and has bought a little time. Matt texted me a few minutes ago that he's meeting with Jake today to try to work out a strategy, but there's not much more Matt or Jake can do to hold them off. The authorities have Dominion, as well as the reports from the Coast Guard and Navy. They know by now that something serious is going on and have gotten some details from Dominion, I'm sure."

Isobel nodded and replied, "In my experience, those government agencies smell blood in the water just like sharks. And they don't like anything to happen under their noses that they aren't privy to. Jake and Ghost are ex-operatives, which perks their ears up even more. I don't know about you, but I need to digest all this and get a bite to eat. It's about lunchtime, and I have some yummy salad fixings. Interested?"

"I sure am. If I don't get some food in my stomach, I'll be drunk. Can't afford to be out of it right now with all that's going on. Listen, Isobel … thank you for being here for me and listening. I don't know what I would do without you. You've always been there for me, no matter what."

"And I will *always* be there for you as long as I am on this planet and even when I'm not. You think I do a lot for you, but what you don't understand is how much you have given to me. You are a bright spot in my life when it was beginning to dim. Since your grandfather passed, I was left with beautiful surroundings and money but no one to share it with. You energized me and gave me purpose again. So, perhaps we have helped each other in equal measure."

Isobel and Kelli stood and embraced, basking in each other's love, warmth, and energy, grateful to have one another.

"Come on, little one. Let's grab some grub."

"Got my favorite dressing?"

"The raspberry vinaigrette is in the fridge. Excuse me just a moment. I have to make a phone call. You go ahead and get started."

CHAPTER 45

Matt's Bungalow
Anna Maria Island, Florida

"Those were good sandwiches, Jake. Make 'em yourself?" Matt asked.

"Actually, I did. Bought some good stuff at the deli and decided to throw it all together in a Dagwood sandwich."

"A Dagwood sandwich? You're dating yourself there, buddy. Heard from Ghost?"

"Got a text message asking if we got here safely and if I had heard from our previous employers? I messaged him back that we got here with no problem but that I have already been approached by our old handler."

"They didn't waste any time, did they?"

"Not those guys. Once they get a sniff of something they think might be of value to the Agency, they move on it."

"How much did you tell them?"

"Didn't have to tell them too much. As we suspected, they already knew about some of the skirmishes we were in and had seen the Coast Guard incident reports as well as the one from the Navy. And now they have Dominion and our nine-fingered buddy in custody. I guarantee you they're working them both over pretty good. They're also getting a lot of heat from some of the jurisdictions who are complaining that we shit in their nests. Like Collier County and Miami-Dade. Maybe even the Bimini authorities. I owned up to our role in the different incidents, but of course, they wanted to know why these guys were so hell-bent on killing us and what we were after that was so important.”

Jake continued, “At this point, I can assure you they’re going to ask us questions they already have gotten answers to from interrogating Dominion and Camel Turd. They will cross-check their answers against ours to see who is telling the truth—oldest tactic in the business. I tried to play it off as you having inherited some sketchy treasure maps from your grandfather and that Dominion thought there was some money to be made, but they didn’t buy that for a minute. They know there’s more to this story, and I can’t convince them otherwise. I don’t think you can either. They already know too much.”

Matt took a sip of his soda, chewed on his lip, and considered Jake’s line of thinking. It was hard to argue with, but Matt would not just roll over after all they had been through, give them everything they want, and walk away like it never happened. He had to find a way to maintain control of the storage crystals and still stay out of jail. But, even if he ended up in jail, he had to make sure nobody from the government got possession of the crystals.

“I hear what you’re saying, and I don’t know what *you* plan to do, but I’m going to face your friends head-on. I’ll answer their questions to a point, but when it comes to telling them the deeper details about what we found or where they’re hidden, I won’t do it. I’ll claim the items are just historical artifacts and none of their business. I discovered them, and I own them.”

Jake stared at his friend, dropped his gaze to the half-eaten sandwich laying on the wrapper, and shook his head.

Old buddy, you don’t know what you’re getting yourself into with these guys. This is the big leagues.

Jake raised his tired eyes back to Matt’s resolute face and decided to make another run at restoring his friend’s sanity.

“Listen carefully to me. I get your need to protect this stuff. And I wish I could help you do that. But you need to understand who these people are that you’re going to be dealing with. They won’t play nice for very long, and they sure as hell won’t play fair. I’m betting they already know these artifacts have strategic value and they need to be the first ones to know what that value is. Once they are convinced this is a matter of national security, they will stop at nothing to get the truth out of us and take possession of the artifacts. They're as ruthless as Dominion in their own way. But this time, there won't be anyone coming to save you or me or any of us. These guys have the resources of the entire U. S. government, military, and intelligence organizations at their disposal. There's no escape once they're on your tail, and they do *not* accept no for an answer. Trust me on this."

"I still have my rights, don't I? I'm an American citizen and subject to due process under the law. So, if they take me into custody, I'll call a good lawyer and drag this thing out. Maybe I can get a story out to the press about false imprisonment or something to get them to back off."

Jake could not help but chuckle at Matt's naiveté. "I'm sorry to have to tell you this, Pardner, but when it comes to matters of national security, there is no due process. I assure you that Dominion and Mr. Jihad aren't enjoying any constitutional rights, and they will declare you a threat to national security and suspend your rights, too. These guys operate both inside and outside the law. They have to in order to do the shit jobs they're tasked with. I know. I was one of them. But sometimes, they abuse that privilege, though, in their eyes, this is not one of those times. They will see you as a genuine threat to our national interests if you don't come clean. They will classify you as a rogue agent in possession of dangerous information that could be weaponized against the U. S. and its allies. They can frame your actions any way they choose, and they can make it stick."

"What are *you* going to do, Jake?"

Jake looked at Matt with conflict and pain etched into his face and eyes. He looked down at the kitchen table, rapped his knuckles on the tabletop a few times, and locked eyes with Matt again.

"Look, Matt, I've done all I can to protect you and these crystals. You know that. And in any other situation, I would continue to do so. But you have to see that I'm stuck between a rock and a hard place right now. I'm being asked to choose between my loyalty to you and the oath I made to the Agency and to this country many years ago. Furthermore, I'm no longer convinced that you or anyone else should be running around with these artifacts where they could be stolen by the wrong people or lost or damaged."

"Jake, I believe the CIA *is* one of those 'wrong people' you're talking about. You know more than anyone what they're capable of. This knowledge needs to be shared with the world, not just one group. Or maybe it shouldn't be shared with anyone at all. I'm not sure we're ready for it."

"Yeah? Good luck with that. How do you do that and maintain control over the information, so it doesn't get used for the wrong reasons by the wrong people down the road? People or governments who are just as bad or worse than Dominion? You don't have those kinds of resources or capability. It's about choosing the lesser of the evils in this scenario. As bad as they might be, the Agency is still a better choice than about anywhere else I can think of for these crystals to end up. And they're capable of protecting them. Hell, look at the alternatives. Terrorist groups, dictatorships, sworn enemies of our country. People like Dominion and his greedy corporate friends. I don't think we can risk letting those kinds of people get their hands on that much power. They would either wipe us off the planet in the blink of an eye or turn us into their slaves. I don't believe that our government would do either of those two."

"So, you're saying you're going to tell them everything you know?"

"Jesus, what else can I do? If I don't, they'll take away everything I've worked for my entire life and charge me with felonies for all that up-close-and-personal work I did on our trip. I wasn't sanctioned to go out and do all that stuff on my own. I broke enough domestic and international laws to nail me with multiple life sentences. We all did. They'll throw my old ass in jail and let me rot there. And, whether you want to accept it or not, they will still get what they want in the end."

Matt hung his head in resignation.

"I understand, and I'm sorry about all this. I really am. Bad situation all around."

"I have no choice. I hope you can see that."

"You always have a choice."

"Maybe I do. But, how about Kelli and Ghost? They'll pick them up for questioning, too. Are you giving them a choice? Is this worth sending us all to prison for? They will apply pressure in ways that you haven't even imagined. Your family will not be untouchable either. These guys have a long reach. NASA? Coast Guard? No place is out of their reach, and they will find your weak spots and exploit them. You have to understand that. What would it do to you to see Kelli get the Guantanamo treatment? Don't think they will use torture? Think again. They know you may not be willing to act to protect yourself, but you *will* act to protect the ones you care about. They will find your soft spot and exploit it, Pardner. They're experts at it."

Matt went numb as the full realization of what Jake had just said sunk in.

CHAPTER 46

Matt's Bungalow
Anna Maria Island, Florida

THE TWO FEDERAL AGENTS, John Milburn and Avery Thompson, sat across the kitchen table from Matt. They had shown up at the beach bungalow mid-morning, the day after Matt's gut-wrenching conversation with Jake. Matt had set his mind to do what he believed he had to do. He knew this was his burden more than anyone else's, and he would take the fall. He had called Kelli and filled her in on the latest developments and what his decision would be. She pleaded with him to think this through and not endanger himself, but to no avail.

In the end, Matt asked her to do him just one more favor—to please hide the crystals the best she could and if it came down to the artifacts being seized by the government, she was to get in her boat and take them out to a deep spot in the Gulf and send them to the bottom. Matt had decided it was better to hide them from the world again than to risk them being used for the wrong purposes.

Matt had thought about this long and hard. In the end, he understood that the information on those storage crystals would force a complete revision of world history, bring into question every religious doctrine, and open the door to a whole new realm of scientific knowledge and technology. This was the hidden history of all mankind, and it belonged to everyone, not just a privileged few. Unless the records contained inside the storage crystals could be shared with all the people in a way that did not create chaos, it would be best to hide them again or even destroy them. They could potentially do more harm than good.

Matt rose from the table to fill his coffee cup and brought the freshly brewed pot of coffee over to fill their mugs as well.

"Sugar? Cream?" Matt asked.

"No thanks, we're good," John replied. "You were in the Navy, so you know how we all get used to drinking our coffee black."

John gave Matt a knowing grin and added, "Where we have to go sometimes, sugar and cream is not always available."

Matt smiled and nodded. He did not resent these agents. They were of the same ilk as his good friend Jake, or at least John was. Their lives were not easy most of the time. He knew they were just doing their jobs and taking orders like most everyone else. It was time to see where this would go.

"Jake briefed me on where things are with you guys, for the most part. I'll tell you what I can. So, let's get it over with."

"Good," John replied. "So, let's cut to the chase. I don't want to draw this out any more than you do. This is not one of the most enjoyable assignments I have ever been on. Jake and I go back a long way and have been through hell together more than I care to remember. He was one of the best I've ever seen. Maybe THE best. And, he was under my guidance and protection as I'm sure he told you by now. The last thing I want to do is come down here and lean on all of you. But that's my job, and if it has to happen, I would rather it be me than someone else who doesn't understand who Jake is and what he has done for this country. By the same token, he is still legally bound to his ex-employer for as long as he lives. Part of the life he and I chose. It's what he signed up for, and he understands the rules of this game. So, if I have to turn the heat up on Jake to get some answers, I will. Refusing to cooperate is not an option for him."

"Alright, dammit! Let's just stop this bullshit right here," Matt flared. "None of that will be necessary. I'm the one that got him into all this, and I want him left out of it. I owe him my life … several times over."

"You and a lot of others, Matt. Many people, including me, are still walking around on this planet because of him. Perhaps, tens of thousands of lives have been saved due to the work he has done behind the scenes. I will be more than happy to let Jake get back to his marina and leave him in peace if you cooperate. God knows he's earned it."

"And you won't go after Ghost or my girlfriend or other friends or relatives?"

"Not if you tell me what I need to know."

"What *do* you need to know?" Matt asked.

Avery had been standing by watching the two men play footsy and could stand it no more. He was going to burst with rookie fervor if he did not jump in. So he jumped. "We need to know what those things are that you found on Bimini and where the hell they are right now or … or else!"

John wheeled on Avery with a withering look that might have killed some men. He stood up and glared down at his associate, hovering over him like a mama grizzly bear about to devour a threat to her cubs.

"You listen to me, Thompson, and you listen good. You better start showing some respect here, or I'll personally kick your Ivy League ass until you can't sit down for a week. These men are not thugs and criminals. They are not the enemy. You have seen Jake's service records, and Matt is a veteran of Naval Intelligence. They were putting their lives on the line for this country while you were still a gleam in your daddy's eye or popping pimples. You can only hope to be the men they are. This is exactly why I personally chose to take this assignment so young, wet-behind-the-ears, Johnny-come-lately, know-it-all dicks like you wouldn't come down here like Nazi stormtroopers and treat these good men like shit. Got it?"

"Yes, sir."

"You better. The next time you open your mouth, you'll find yourself in the ER having my shoe removed from your rectum!"

Matt was surprised and moved by the loyalty and respect displayed by John. *But wait a minute … was this a good cop and bad cop routine?* He was not sure, but it mattered little. He was going to have to deal with John, regardless.

"Sorry for my associate's rudeness. He's a little impatient and overzealous perhaps. Still has a lot to learn," John offered. "But though he could have been more polite about it, his question is valid. Do you care to address it?"

"To a point. Can you tell me what interest the United States government has in any historical artifacts that I may possess?"

"Well, normally we wouldn't have much interest in such a thing. But our investigation has led us to believe that these are not your typical historical relics. In fact, Mr. Dominion has informed us that through his own investigation, he became convinced that these artifacts contain the records of an ancient civilization and keys to very advanced technologies. That is why he pursued you so heavily. He believes whoever possesses the knowledge contained in these artifacts will, in fact, control the future of the world. I think you can see how that would be a matter of interest to our government, don't you? What do you think of Dominion's theory?"

"It's obvious that Mr. Dominion is a deranged man, John. Nobody in their right mind would do the things he did even if that individual believed these relics contained valuable information. So, I don't care to comment on Dominion's beliefs."

"Okay, what do *you* believe these artifacts can tell us if we were to study them?" John asked.

"I don't know that I'm qualified to answer that. The information they hold is written in an unknown language that would require years of translation and interpretation before anyone could determine its value. Since that is the case, I don't understand why I can't be free to study my discoveries like other academics and scholars would do."

"But, who better to bring all those resources to bear than the agencies of the U. S. government? If there's nothing of strategic importance found on the artifacts, then they would be released back into your sole possession. What is your objection to that?"

"Because they are *my* discovery, that I made, using my own resources, and I choose to have them studied under my supervision without interference or oversight from outside parties."

"I hate to pull the State Department card Matt, but in reality, those artifacts would be viewed as property of the Bahamian government. It is my understanding that they were unaware of your activities as a visitor to their island, and furthermore, do not take kindly to tourists ripping off their historical treasures. So, any way you look at it, you can't keep them. Your only decision is whether you will turn them over to us or return them to the government of the Bahamas. If you choose to give them back to the people of the Bahamas, I can assure you we will end up with them anyway. That deal has already been put in place. So, the smart thing to do is agree to let us have them for a while and see if this whole thing is really such a big deal. In return for your cooperation, we would let you and everyone involved here get back to their normal lives without interference. We would also tie up the loose ends you left behind in multiple legal jurisdictions. Do you not agree that would be a reasonable solution for all involved?"

Matt felt the noose tightening. He was running out of wiggle room. "What if I file a lawsuit claiming custody? After all, it was my grandfather who originally discovered these items. Would you not have to back off until the lawsuit is settled?"

John allowed himself a slight smile as he considered Matt's ploy.

"Nice try, but your grandfather never made a public claim that he discovered these artifacts or had any knowledge of them. Truth is, we would classify these artifacts as part of a terrorist plot by Dominion and Kabil and seize them as part of that ongoing investigation. Anyone who chose to stand in the way and not cooperate with that seizure of evidence would be viewed as a possible accessory and charged with obstructing a federal investigation, obstruction of justice, and aiding and abetting a known terrorist. It would be a lot easier if you would just allow us to examine your artifacts and get it over with. There really is no other option."

"I'm sure it would be the easier route, but I'm just not feelin' it yet. Can I have some time to think about it?"

A little redness started to show on John's countenance, and Matt could see that he was pushing this thing to critical mass.

"Yes. You can have until 1700 today to decide. However, you will be under surveillance from now until then. Additional law enforcement personnel will be stationed at your house as well as the surrounding area. Meanwhile, I may have to pay another visit to our mutual friend, Jake. Perhaps he can shed a little more light on this matter."

"You agreed to leave everyone else alone?" Matt said.

"That promise was made in exchange for your full cooperation. And so far, that's just not happening."

"Okay … Okay. Just please leave Jake and the rest of them out of this. This is my problem, and I need to take care of it myself."

"My preference as well. Now, please be kind enough to produce the artifacts, and we'll be on our way."

"Uh … there's a bit of a problem with that. They're not here."

"Then, where are they?"

"I can't say."

"Can't say or won't say?"

"I really can't say. I don't know the exact whereabouts of the relics at this time."

"What? What kind of bullshit answer is that? You mean to tell me that you don't know where they are after all this talk about protecting them?"

"Strange, but true."

"You must know I don't believe that for a minute? You leave me no choice but to take you and your friends into custody and see who knows what. I know where to find Jake and Ghost. Care to tell me where to find Miss Renner?"

"Not really."

"Doesn't matter. We have a locator beacon on her vehicle and a GPS fix on her phone. I just wanted to see what you would say. You didn't really think we would come to this party unprepared, did you?"

Matt tensed, and his mind raced. *I have to warn Kelli.*

"Oh, and by the way, Matt. Your phone is bugged, too. We already knew about your failsafe plan to ditch the artifacts. Hand me your phone, please."

Matt handed it over without a struggle. He could never complete a call or message before these two would react. It was beginning to look like it had all been for nothing. He was out of options and out of ideas. Kelli would never have enough warning now to get rid of the storage crystals. They are probably watching her anyway and would never allow it to happen.

What the hell ever made me think I could pull this off? I'm so sorry Grandpa … I tried my best … I really did.

Matt stood while the agents cuffed his hands in front of him and led him out to their car, where they situated him in the back seat. He was glad no neighbors were outside to witness him being taken into custody. They had been traumatized enough when the news got out that someone had broken into Matt's house and tried to murder him.

What would they think if they saw him being taken away in restraints and put in the back of an official vehicle?

As the black sedan pulled away, Matt turned and looked back through the rear window at his little beach bungalow and wondered if he would ever see it again, feeling a deep, biting sadness over losing the near-perfect life he had enjoyed such a short time ago.

And when would he see Kelli again?

CHAPTER 47

Jake's Marina
Anna Maria Island, Florida

"We can do this the easy way or the hard way, as you used to like to say," John stated.

Jake looked around the perimeter of the marina office and could see through the windows that the building was surrounded by Feds and local law enforcement. He glanced back over his shoulder and saw two men with their weapons drawn and blocking his escape route through the doorway to the shop.

"Guess Matt didn't give you what you wanted, huh?" Jake said with a slight chuckle.

"Sorry, Jake. We need our answers. You understand how this works."

"Yeah, unfortunately, I do."

Jake was firmly clasped into handcuffs and led without incident to a waiting black sedan.

He looked back through the rear window of the car as it sped away and wondered if he would ever see his beloved marina again. He turned back around, facing forward in his seat, set his jaw, and prepared for the worst.

CHAPTER 48

Ghost's Safe House
Johnson's Ridge, Kentucky

GHOST SLOWED DOWN TO make the turn into his driveway. He had driven to Morehead to pick up some groceries and other odds and ends and was now returning home, looking forward to a good dinner and relaxing on his back deck with a glass of Kentucky bourbon, straight up, on the rocks. Sippin' whiskey he called it. He might even give a call to that good-looking brunette college professor that had moved in down the road to see what her plans were for the evening. He had run into her a few times at the nearby country store, and she had hinted about them getting together as she was new to the area and wanted to make new friends. *Might be an interesting evening.*

He had just started to make the left-hand turn when suddenly, without warning, cars converged on him from every direction, tires screeching and blocking any escape route he could have used. There were two black government sedans and three Kentucky State Police cruisers. A bullhorn blared for him to step out of the car and keep his hands in the air.

What the hell is going on here?

He did not have a clue what this was all about, but it had to be a dumb mistake. He decided to play it safe and comply … for the moment. He would straighten it out once he knew who was behind this. Ghost slowly exited the Jeep, keeping his hands in plain view of the officers.

A familiar figure emerged from the black sedan directly in front of him.

Damned if it wasn't Tom Reed, one of his old handlers at the Shop. He looked a little older and more world-weary than the last time he had seen him, but Tom's commanding presence and twinkling eyes remained.

"Tom … really? What the hell are you doing here, and what's with all the drama? If you wanted to come visit, all you had to do was call," Ghost said.

"I'm afraid you would not have welcomed my visit under these circumstances. I *did* come to see you, Ghost. Though, I wish it was for fun instead of business."

"What's this all about?"

"I'm afraid I have to take you in to the Agency for questioning."

"Questioning about what?"

"About that recent tropical cruise you took. We know a lot of what happened, and we have already taken Jake and the others in for questioning as well. We need to fill in some holes in the story and tie up the loose ends. You guys left quite a trail of destruction. You also involved government agencies on several occasions. You already know we have Dominion and his partner in custody. Thanks for handing that terrorist sonofabitch over to us. They tell me that you all had a bang-up party here at your place not long ago. We need some answers, Ghost."

"Can't you just ask your questions here?"

"No can do. The Agency has decided it would be best to round all of you up and bring you back to the Shop for debriefing. It will be much easier to work through this thing that way. Plus, we don't want any runners to deal with … if you get my drift."

"Can I put my groceries away first?"

"I think it would be best if you just got in the car with me right now and forget about the groceries. You are one of the best operatives I ever worked with, and I don't want to give you time to be tempted into pulling any of your tricks. Let's just keep it civil, okay? I don't want any harm to come to you or Jake or any of your friends. But to be honest, the Agency has a lot of things they can use as leverage against all of you, and I don't want to see them have to use it. Fair enough?"

Ghost looked around at the manpower arrayed against him and thought about the threats his former handler was hinting at. He knew Tom was telling the truth. That was how the Agency operated. They always found a way to get what they wanted.

The best thing I can do right now is to stay calm, cooperate, and see where this leads. Hopefully, they will get what they want and go away. I don't see any way Matt will be able to hang onto those relics now. Damn shame …

"Alright, Tom. Can I give this bag of groceries to someone, so they don't go to waste? Somebody should take them home and use them."

"Yeah, make it quick. We have a plane waiting."

Ghost opened the back hatch to the Jeep and lifted out a full bag of groceries. He turned toward the officers and agents gathered around him.

"Well, who wants some free grub to take home to their family? There are ribeyes and ice cream and all kinds of goodies in here."

One of the younger state troopers gave him a nod and eagerly stepped forward to take the bag. Ghost decided to give these good ol' boys a little entertainment before he left.

Instead of handing the bag to the officer, he tossed the groceries to him. Acting out of instinct, the trooper lunged forward with open arms to catch the bag. Everyone was watching the flight of the grocery sack, and before they could blink or move, Ghost had flashed around behind the surprised trooper and had him in a headlock that would have allowed him to snap the man's neck if he so chose. Everyone froze, shocked at the speed at which the situation had changed and unsure what to do next. Ghost stared around at all of them with a look of pure calm and deadly focus. The officers now understood what they were dealing with. Ice water ran in Ghost's veins. Most of the lawmen were from around the area and had heard stories. Seemed the stories were true.

Ghost held the situation for a few moments to create the maximum chilling effect, then relaxed his hold on the trooper, patted him on the shoulder, smiled toward Tom, and stepped back with his hands out for cuffing.

"Good catch, trooper. If you had dropped those groceries, I would've been real upset. I was raised poor, and I hate to see good food go to waste," Ghost said, still grinning.

The trooper still had not moved and was looking back and forth between the grocery sack and Ghost.

"Why the hell did you have to pull that little stunt, you damned showoff?" Tom asked, suppressing a smile as he placed handcuffs around Ghost's wrists.

"Because I can," Ghost replied. "I didn't want you to think I'd gone soft and lost my edge. If I didn't want to go, you know I wouldn't be going. You didn't bring enough men."

"Yeah, I know. I appreciate you not making this more difficult on me than it already is. I would rather have taken a beating than have to come up here and get you."

The onlookers were still watching in stunned silence with their hands resting on their sidearms, just in case. After cuffing Ghost, Tom helped him into the passenger seat of his black sedan rather than forcing him into the back where they normally seat wrongdoers. He shut the passenger door, walked around the front of the car, opened his driver door, and stopped to look at the agents and officers around him.

"Gentlemen, know this. This man is one of the best of the best. He wasn't kidding. If he didn't want to go today, it would have taken a lot more of us to make him do it. That's why they sent me. They hoped that because Ghost and I have a long history, I could work this out peacefully. Don't even think of looking at this man like he's a criminal. He's a hero in every sense of the word and has done more to keep this country secure than all of you will ever do in all your lifetimes put together. He is to be treated accordingly while he is in our custody, or you will answer to me. Am I clear?"

All nodded.

After settling into the front passenger seat of the black government sedan, Ghost barely noticed the engine revving and the car moving forward. He looked back over his left shoulder through the rear window at his retirement homestead disappearing from view and wondered if he would ever see it again.

CHAPTER 49

Isobel's Estate
Bird Key, Florida

JOHN MILBURN ADVANCED WITH caution toward the waterfront estate of Isobel Renner. He did not want to attract any more attention than necessary. This was a neighborhood where rock stars, bestselling novelists, and famous TV personalities spent their winters, and they would not take kindly to having their corner of paradise invaded by government agents creating a ruckus. He radioed the other two backup cars to follow his lead and to not do anything out of the ordinary or alarm the residents if at all possible.

John parked his sedan down the street from the main gate to the sprawling estate, making certain that his car would be out of sight to anyone in the big house. He got out of the car, took a look at the handcuffed guest in the back seat, threatened to put a gag in Matt's mouth if he opened it, and signaled the two cars behind him to park to the rear of his position. The four agents in those vehicles joined him on the palm-lined avenue leading to the front security gate of the majestic home. They paused while John produced a cell phone from his belt holster. He pushed a preset button on the face of the phone and waited for an answer.

"This is John Milburn. We are at our destination on Bird Key. Have you contacted the security company with our court order and obtained those gate codes for me yet?

"Very good. Text them to me as soon as we terminate this call."

He punched the End Call button and waited for the text to come through. As soon as it showed up, he opened it and read the digits that would give him driveway access to the mansion in front of him.

"Stay close, gentlemen. Let's do this fast and quiet. No unnecessary force is to be used. There should only be two women inside, so let's act appropriately unless challenged. They are only wanted for questioning at this time and are not charged with any crimes."

John approached the entrance and stood in front of the keypad. He entered the security code and watched the ornate iron gates swing wide open. He and his agents passed through at a jog and paused before reaching the front door. He sent two men to the rear of the house and told the remaining agents to hold this position at the front of the house. John and Avery walked up to the imposing front doors and knocked. Nobody came to the door, and no sounds could be heard from within. John pulled his comm unit from its belt clip and used it to ask the agents in the rear if they could see or hear anyone. The answer was negative.

John knocked again and waited. Nothing. He rang the doorbell and listened to the melodious chimes playing an upbeat tune inside the main entry hall. Still no response. Well, he had tried to be courteous, but unfortunately, it never seemed to work out that way.

He reached out, gripped the large, brass door handle, and cautiously twisted it. It did not resist. Much to his surprise, the door was unlocked. He found that strange in a house such as this, where security is usually a high priority. He motioned for the agents in front to move up to a position on each side of the front door and hold there. He radioed the agents in back that he was entering from the front and instructed them to try the back door to see if it was unlocked. If so, they were to enter and meet him and Avery inside.

John slowly pushed open the right side of the large double doors. He warily advanced into the main foyer with Avery close on his heels. He paused and listened, but it was as quiet as an empty church.

"Hello, is anyone here? My name is John Milburn, and I am here on behalf of the U. S. government. We are here to speak with Kelli Renner. Ms. Renner, if you are here, please show yourself."

The only sound that could be heard was that of the stately grand-father clock ticking in the foyer. John looked around at the double staircase leading to the second floor and the magnificent chandelier that was suspended over their heads. He shook his head in amazement. It hung from the second-floor ceiling to a point no more than twelve feet from the floor on which he was standing, perfectly dividing the two-story atrium between the impressive curved staircases. *Hell, that chandelier probably cost more than I paid for my whole damned house back in Virginia.*

John heard sounds ahead, and the two agents who had been stationed in the rear of the house now appeared before him.

"Did you see anyone or anything of interest?" John asked.

"No, sir. The back door was open, so we searched the whole south and west side of the house and found nothing."

"Okay … you guys check the garage, and we'll look upstairs." John instructed.

John climbed the staircase on the left and Avery the one on the right. The stairways converged again at the second-floor landing. They combed their way through the multiple bedrooms, closets, baths, and sitting rooms on the second story. They identified Kelli's room by the pictures and memorabilia displayed there. Much to their surprise, a cell phone battery was placed openly on a nightstand beside the bed so they could find it. *Damn, I bet this is Kelli Renner's phone battery. She must have figured out we might track her cell phone. So much for finding her that way.*

Further down the hallway and taking up the whole southwest corner of the upstairs was the master suite. The master bedroom and Kelli's room, as well as the other guest rooms, were immaculate. No clutter. No sign of recent habitation. Beds made. Closet doors closed. Bath towels folded neatly and dry to the touch. John and Avery headed back downstairs.

"What did you find in the garage?" John asked the agents.

"Nothing out of the ordinary other than the fact that Kelli Renner's pickup truck is inside as well as a Bentley convertible with Isobel Renner's name on the registration. If they're not here, they didn't leave in their own vehicles. Neither vehicle has been used recently. The engines are cold."

John analyzed what they had found so far. Front and back doors were left open. Both vehicles were in the garage.

Surely, they couldn't have known we were coming. We had confiscated Matt's cell phone, so he couldn't have made any calls that would have warned them we were on our way. We also monitored Jake's phone, and he didn't call Kelli either. Ghost didn't know this was going down, so he couldn't have warned anyone. Isobel Renner keeps her boat at the Sarasota Yacht Club, and it's still docked there, so they couldn't have used it to get away. Kelli Renner's boat is still docked at her business location in Siesta Key.

Damn! This doesn't make any sense.

John pulled his cell phone out again and hit a preset.

"We found no occupants at the Bird Key location. No sign of either of them. House was unlocked and cars in the garage. I need a forensics team down here ASAP. I want the entire house searched thoroughly, and fingerprints lifted anywhere you can find them. Have them look for ancient artifacts or anything unusual that may be on the property. Bring in ground penetrating radar to search the grounds for hiding places. You can get a microwave and FLIR team in here as well to look through walls and floors for places where something can be stashed. I need to know who has been here, and I would sure as hell like to know where these two have disappeared to."

"We'll get those teams assembled and on the way immediately, sir."

"See that you do."

John and Avery walked back out to the street and approached the car where Matt was being detained.

"Where's Kelli?" Matt asked.

"You tell me, smartass!" John shot back.

Matt started laughing. "You mean she's not there?"

"No, she's not. Why don't you save us a lot of aggravation and time and give us some ideas of where she and her grandmother might have run off to?"

Matt was still laughing. Relief pouring out through his laughter. *I'll be damned! Kelli and Isobel have gotten away somehow. I always knew Isobel was a sharp cookie. Wonder where they went? What their plan is?*

Matt's cathartic giggling finally subsided, and he looked up at John and Avery, trying to look serious.

"Well, guys, I can honestly say that I don't have a clue where they are. I know those two are way too smart to pick somewhere obvious that you would have under surveillance. So, you can hook me up to a polygraph or whatever you want to do, but I can't help you."

John stared a hole through Matt. He was not accustomed to being outmaneuvered. Especially by civilians and amateurs.

"Alright, hotshot. Have it your way. Maybe a trip to the Shop will jog your memory."

John and Avery climbed into the front of the car, and John gunned it away from the curb and down the perfectly manicured boulevard, leaving the other agents behind to secure the premises.

John looked in the rearview mirror at Matt and scowled.

"Go on and enjoy this little game you're playing. Let's see how much you enjoy the games they will have planned for you at Langley."

CHAPTER 50

Isobel's Estate
Bird Key, Florida
The Night before the Roundup

Isobel ended the call she had made on her cell phone.

"Here's what we're going to do, Kelli. We're going to pack a few belongings, including those artifacts you have, and we're going to go away for a while."

"Why? What's going on?"

"Let's just say that I have been informed by a reliable source that we will be getting some unwanted guests coming by soon."

"You mean the CIA?"

"I believe so. You know they've been circling all of you like barracudas, and it seems we're the next stop on their fishing expedition. They will be coming to take us and your artifacts into custody. They are already in the process of picking up your other three friends, including Matt."

"Isobel, how do you know all this? Do you work for the government or something?"

Isobel laughed heartily and shook her head. Her eyes danced and she looked ten years younger.

"No, no, no, my child. Nothing so sinister as that. I just happen to have some well-placed friends you might say, and they have my best interests at heart … and yours."

"How long do we have before they get here? And where are we going?"

"Where we are going is not for you to worry about, my dear one. Just know that it will be a safe place where they cannot reach you. We will be among old friends of mine. I don't think the government men will come to get us until tomorrow morning, but just in case, we will leave today as soon as we can pack."

"Then, how do we get where we're going? Are we driving?"

"Again … it is all taken care of. My friends have sent a car and will arrange our transportation from that point on."

"Should I pack for warm weather or cold?"

"Just pack for comfort. It will not be cold enough for heavy clothing. I think an extra jacket will do. If we need additional items, they will be provided."

Kelli stood very still and looked at Isobel with searching eyes as if there should be something else she should ask her. This seemed as strange as all the other events that had taken place over the last few weeks.

"Isobel, is there something I should know? This all seems very unusual to me. Especially after all the crazy things I've seen lately."

Isobel smiled warmly, walked over to Kelli, and held her gently in her arms, just like she did when Kelli was small.

"My dear Kelli, you are everything to me. You need to remember that, no matter what happens. There are many things you need to know. And, some of them you will come face-to-face with very soon. But, don't be alarmed at my words. The things you will come to know are good things. Wonderful things. It is time for you to learn some higher truths."

"Higher truths? What are you—?"

"Come dear. Time's wasting, and we need to prepare for our journey. There will be plenty of time for questions and answers later. For now, we have to gather our things. Our ride will be here in less than two hours, and we must be ready. Did you turn off your cellphone and take out the battery? Our friends in the government have gained access to it and have been using it to track you."

"Yes, I did, but how did you know they were tracking me through it?"

"Let's go, Miss Kelli. All will be answered. The only thing you need to worry about right now is to make sure you pack matching outfits!"

Isobel giggled and moved off to her bedroom upstairs. Kelli watched her climb the staircase and marveled at her energy, youthful spirit, iron will, intellect, and endless sense of mystery.

Something tells me my life is never going to be the same again after today. What in the heavens has my grandmother been keeping from me all these years? Guess I'm about to find out …

CHAPTER 51

Interrogation Room 5
CIA Headquarters
Langley, Virginia

JOHN MILBURN STOOD BEFORE Amir Kabil and his two colleagues who had been found asleep on the floor of the house where they had held Carol Flannery hostage. The three detainees were sitting in metal chairs on one side of a long, gray steel table. They were bound by hand and ankle cuffs that were secured to steel loops embedded in the concrete floor of the room. The harsh illumination in the small space came from a couple of rows of overhead neon tubes with no covers to diffuse and soften the light. There was nothing on the walls other than a United States Central Intelligence Agency logo plaque. There was a single door into the room and a long reflective window on one side for outside observers to see through without being seen. Milburn stared ominously at his captives for close to a full minute before breaking his gaze and slowly taking a seat opposite them at the table.

"We have questioned you individually, and we have a fairly clear picture of your involvement in the kidnapping of Mrs. Flannery and subsequent attacks in Kentucky on the other four individuals. By the way, how did that situation in Kentucky work out for you, Mr. Kabil?" Milburn asked with a slight smirk.

"Those crazy men killed my brothers and cut off one of my fingers."

Milburn chuckled. "I believe that was your trigger finger if I'm not mistaken. You are fortunate to have escaped with your life, Mr. Kabil. You were sent on a fool's errand by Dominion."

"Who were those men who tortured me?" Kabil asked.

"Let's just say they are special and leave it at that," Milburn replied. "There is one area we are still a little fuzzy on. The part where you two, Mr. X and Mr. Y, fell asleep on guard duty and allowed your hostage to escape. Can you enlighten me on that particular part of the story so we can finish up here? How did that happen and who liberated Mrs. Flannery?"

Mr. X and Mr. Y looked at each other with perplexed faces. They also glanced at Kabil, who was staring at them with obvious condemnation over their failure to guard the hostage.

Mr. X spoke. "We do not know. That is the truth. Everyone says we fell asleep on duty, but we did not. We both remember playing cards and telling jokes, but we were not sleepy. We had been drinking energy drinks to make sure we stayed awake. We helped our guest relieve herself and went back to the table to play cards again. I remember seeing Mrs. Flannery getting sleepy. The next thing we know, we are in handcuffs being revived with a medical shot. That is all we know. I swear it. May Allah be our witness."

"It is true that it took a stimulant to revive you both," Milburn replied. "That wouldn't have been necessary if you were just napping on the job. But the strange part is no sleeping drugs, or any other drugs were found after we tested your blood. So, that ruled out the theory that someone doctored your drinks or food. Did anyone else visit the house after you took Mrs. Flannery there?"

"No. It was forbidden. We did not want anyone to lead the police to that house. There were no other visitors."

"We have been analyzing your voice patterns as you speak, and they confirm that you are more than likely telling the truth."

"I promise you, it is the truth. Amir … we did not fail you. We did not fall asleep that night. I swear by Allah and all that is holy and good. We do not know what happened to us."

Amir studied their faces for a few moments and could see the sincerity in their eyes. He believed them. *But if that is true … what did happen that night?*

"I believe you, brothers. Do not feel bad. It is me who failed you and Allah," Amir replied.

"Okay, that's enough 'I'm okay, You're okay' talk," Milburn interrupted. "You've had your feel-good moment. Anyway, it's not Allah you should be worried about right now. You will all face a military tribunal on international terrorism charges. My guess is you will never see the outside world again."

John Milburn stepped out into the hall and nodded for the Marines on duty to take the men to their holding cells. He watched as they were removed from the room, still puzzled by the curious state that Mr. X and Mr. Y had been found in. Mrs. Flannery had also displayed the same condition.

Who in the hell could have rendered those three people unconscious without a struggle and without being observed? And without the use of drugs? They had to be "good guys" … didn't they? After all, they returned Mrs. Flannery to her home and put her in bed unharmed.

Milburn shook his head and looked to find Avery.

"Come on, Avery. We have a lot of work to do. We have more guests to interview."

CHAPTER 52

Isobel's Estate
Bird Key, Florida

Isobel and Kelli had finished packing and were now standing in the expansive foyer near the front doors.

"Do you have everything you need, dear?" Isobel asked.

"I think so. I wasn't exactly sure how to pack for my magical mystery tour," Kelli quipped.

"Not to worry. You will want for nothing, I promise."

"Well, that's good to know. I was worried we would be hiding out in a hut in a jungle somewhere. Or maybe a cave."

"People do tend to imagine the worst when faced with the unknown. But you should know me well enough to understand that any cave I would hide out in would be well appointed," Isobel said with a playful smile on her face.

"You don't seem to be too worried about all this?"

"That's because there's nothing to worry about. We will be in very good hands for as long as we need to stay out of sight."

"You feel that confident, even with the CIA after me? They're not so easy to hide from, you know?"

"That's true. But all I can tell you right now is that my friends are monitoring the situation and making sure that you and I are one step ahead of our friends in Langley."

"Are you sure you weren't a spy or something?"

"I assure you, I have never been in the employ of any government on this earth in any capacity. Now, I think I hear a car outside. Let's get moving."

The two women stepped through the big double doors and out onto the tiled portico, Isobel making sure to leave the front door unlocked behind her just as she had done with the back door. *No sense in having people break in and damage a perfectly beautiful door.* Waiting in front of them was a gleaming, black limousine. Not the type you rent for prom night. A man dressed in a dark, tailored suit, crisp white shirt, and black tie emerged from the driver's compartment and walked to the rear of the car. He looked more like a Marine than a chauffeur to Kelli. He opened the trunk and reached for their bags.

"Good Evening, Mrs. Renner … and Miss Renner."

"Good Evening to you, Mr. Hanson. It's good to see you again," Isobel replied.

"Thank you, Mrs. Renner. It's always a pleasure to see you. I will be your driver and escort for this part of the trip."

"Wonderful!" Isobel said. "You've always been my favorite."

"I've heard a rumor that you say that to all of us," Hanson replied. Hanson looked at Isobel and flashed a big grin. "But I know that I really *am* your favorite."

"Of course, you are," Isobel replied coyly as if everyone would know that.

After carefully placing their bags in the voluminous trunk, he opened both back doors and gestured to the ladies to take their seats inside the spacious limousine. Kelli hesitated to get in and was still holding the backpack that contained the relics. She looked nervously at Isobel, unsure what to do with it.

Isobel said, "It's alright, dear. You can keep them beside you on the seat if you would like. I know how important they are to you."

Once the passengers were situated, Hanson closed the doors softly and returned to the driver's seat.

"Isobel, there's a United States Senate license plate on this car," Kelli said.

"Well, imagine that!" Isobel said with feigned surprise. "Just relax and enjoy the ride, Kelli. We're in good hands with Hanson. He really is my favorite."

Kelli stared at her grandmother as the car wound its way out the gate and toward the unknown. *Who is this woman I know as Isobel?*

CHAPTER 53

Interrogation Room 2
CIA Headquarters
Langley, Virginia

JOHN MILBURN SAT ACROSS the table from Matt Flannery in an interrogation room identical to the one he had just left. Avery Thompson stood in the corner. Matt had been given a bottle of water and was sipping on it. His handcuffs had been removed. John did not consider him a threat with no baseball bat in the room and those Marines parked outside the door.

"Well, what's it going to be, Matt? Are we going to dance all night, or will you give me something I can use to satisfy my bosses so we can call it a day? Then, I'll see about getting you and your two buddies released."

"You know what I know by now. And, I don't have a clue as to where Kelli and the artifacts are. You know I don't. We were both at Isobel's house. I was as surprised as you were. You've already asked me this question while I was hooked to a polygraph and a voice stress analyzer, so you know I'm being truthful. And, I don't know why you're holding Ghost and Jake. They know less than I do, which would be nothing."

"Perhaps. But we felt it would be best to keep all of you where we can talk face-to-face until we make some sense of this. If you can't tell me where the artifacts are, at least tell me what makes them so valuable? Dominion told us he believes they hold the key to ancient technologies that would revolutionize the world. Is that true? And if it is, why would you want to keep it for yourself and not share it with the world? Do you really think you're in a position to protect and develop strategic information and technology such as that? Or are you thinking of becoming another Dominion and building your own little dynasty?"

Matt took a drink of water and slowly twisted the cap back onto the bottle. He put the bottle down on the table and laid it on its side. He twirled the bottle like a pinwheel a couple of times and looked up at John.

"I am not qualified to say if what Dominion told you is true or not. What I saw was interesting, but the information was in a foreign language. So, I don't know exactly what can be gained from those relics. But if it *is* true, I don't want *any* government or organization to get their hands on it. This world is dangerous enough as it is. And, that last question you asked me doesn't even deserve an answer."

"Are you saying you don't trust your own government to safeguard this knowledge?"

"Oh, I'm sure you would safeguard it, all right. I'm just not sure what you would do with it."

John grinned at Matt.

"Oh, I see. Trying to save the world from itself. Nice. You do know this isn't my first rodeo, right? I was doing this while you were still chasing skirts in high school. I can tell when someone is holding out on me or only telling part of the truth. And that's what I'm sensing from you right now. I don't need a polygraph to know that. You were in Naval Intelligence. You're somewhat aware of our capabilities here."

"Yes, I am. But that doesn't change anything. You can shoot me up with drugs, torture me, or threaten my friends and family, but it won't change the fact that I do *not* know where Kelli and the artifacts are, and I don't know what information is contained in those relics. You're beating a dead horse at this point. None of us know enough about what those artifacts might hold to be of any real help to you."

"That's possible, but I'm not convinced. We *will* decide about your level of truthfulness. If we become convinced you or Jake or Ghost are holding out on us, we will level enough felony charges against all of you to fill a book. And we have plenty of evidence available to make those charges stick. In the meantime, you get to stick around and enjoy our world-famous hospitality here at the Shop. And Matt, we better not find out you've been lying or keeping things from us … especially the whereabouts of your lady friend and those artifacts. It won't go well for you if that happens, or as much as it pains me to say it, for Jake and Ghost either. I would hate to see that happen, and it will all be on you if it does. By the way, Dominion ratted out the Director of Security at Kennedy Space Center where your old man works. The asshole was leaking information to Dominion about NASA operations and was also involved in your mom's kidnapping."

Matt dropped his head, feeling the exhaustion and futility of the situation. He had no way out of this, and he could now see the CIA would continue to use his friends and criminal charges as leverage against him. *I wonder where Kelli is … and if she's alright. God, I miss her.* Part of an old song ran through Matt's mind as John stood and exited the room.

I fell into a burning ring of fire
I went down, down, down while the flames went higher
And it burns, burns, burns … the ring of fire … the ring of fire.

"Ring of Fire"
Johnny Cash

CHAPTER 54

John Milburn's Office
CIA Headquarters
Langley, Virginia

"Yes, Deputy Director. We're using every resource at our disposal to locate Miss Renner and the artifacts."

Pause.

"Yes, I know we're the CIA. I realize that it's embarrassing. I am leading the effort personally."

Pause.

"Yes, that's very clear, sir. I will call Forensics as soon as we finish and will report their findings to you."

Pause.

"I understand. Goodbye."

John Milburn dropped the phone back into its cradle and fell back into his office chair. He pulled out a wrinkled white handkerchief and wiped the sweat from his forehead and temples. The deputy director had not been easy on him. He picked up the phone and punched in the number of the leader of the forensics team stationed at Bird Key.

"Milburn here. What have you found?"

"Nothing out of the ordinary, sir. The only fingerprints we found in the house were from Isobel and Kelli Renner, the cook, and the housekeeping staff."

"What about the surveillance cameras at the front gate and around the house? Does it show the women leaving with anyone?"

"No luck there, I'm afraid. Those cameras were disabled early in the afternoon of the day before you went there and did not show anyone entering or leaving the property after Kelli Renner arrived that morning."

"Did you find anything at all that might help us?"

"Nothing that would indicate what their plans were or where they went."

"Damn it. Okay, thanks. Let me know if you come up with anything at all, no matter how far-fetched or insignificant it might seem."

"Yes, sir. I will keep you informed of any new developments in our investigation."

Milburn dropped the phone into the cradle again, with a little more force than last time. Frustration was building to the bursting point inside of him. He stared at the phone for a few moments and picked up the handset. He punched the button that connected directly to the deputy director's private line, feeling like a man on death row. The deputy director picked up on the other end.

"What have you got for me, Milburn?"

"Nothing yet, sir."

"Look, people don't just disappear off the face of the earth without a trace. How hard can it be to find an old woman and her granddaughter? You're missing something here. Redouble your efforts. Put more pressure on those three you have in custody if need be. Maybe they're still holding out on you. Have Forensics sweep that house and grounds again and have them do the same at the three houses where Jake, Ghost, and Matt Flannery live. There has to be a clue somewhere. If any of this stuff is true about those relics, we cannot afford to have it fall into anyone's hands but ours. This has now been classified as a National Security Priority One Operation. You have the best intelligence services in the world at your disposal, now use them! I want those Renner women found, and sooner rather than later. Got it, Milburn?"

"Yes, sir. We'll pull out all the stops."

"You should've already pulled out all the stops. Next time we talk, I want to hear some good news."

"Yes, sir."

The phone went dead in John Milburn's hand. He rocked back and forth in his chair for several minutes while stroking his chin. He returned the phone to its cradle, rubbed his bloodshot eyes, and stood up.

Time to go back to work.

CHAPTER 55

Senator's Limousine
South Florida

KELLI WAS IMAGINING MATT'S kind, handsome face and missing him terribly. Mostly his eyes and the way he sometimes looked at her with such deep affection. She was startled back to the present by the driver's voice.

"Mrs. Renner, your jet is waiting at Coral Creek, and our ETA is about forty minutes," Hanson said.

"Wonderful, Mr. Hanson!" Isobel replied. "I hope there are cocktails on board. I think Miss Kelli is in dire need of one … or two."

"Of course, there are," Hanson said. "The galley is stocked with food as well."

"The senator's hospitality is boundless and gracious as always," Isobel said.

"He loves your visits above all others, I think," Hanson said. "He considers you family and always tells us to do everything we can to make you comfortable."

"He is such a dear man," Isobel replied.

Kelli watched and listened to the exchange in stunned silence, unable to grasp what was happening at the moment as well as how her life had radically changed over the last few weeks. She wasn't sure if it was for the better or worse. She reached over to the backpack that held the relics and picked it up, clutching it to her chest as if it might link her to Matt somehow. She squeezed her eyes tightly shut in an attempt to block out the world around her for a few moments.

I miss Matt so much. I never knew I could love anyone or anything this deeply. Please, God, let him be safe. I can't stand this feeling of not knowing what is happening to him and not being by his side to help him through it.

Kelli began to feel emotionally overwhelmed, and a tear escaped from the corner of her eye and splashed gently on top of the backpack she was clutching to her chest. The backpack felt like the only thing that was real to her at the moment. The only thing connecting her to Matt and the hours and days they had shared. The dangers they had escaped. The discoveries they had made. The deep bond they had forged.

Isobel could see Kelli was descending into a state of mental and emotional distress. She reached out her hand and touched Kelli gently on her arm.

"Kelli, I know you're having a hard time dealing with all that has happened and all that is happening to you right now. Please tell me, what is bothering you the most?"

Kelli sat quietly for a few moments, blinking back tears and trying to recompose herself. She looked out through the deeply tinted limo window at the passing parade of traffic, palm trees, and bright stucco houses. Nameless, meaningless blurs. She took a deep breath, relaxed her grip on the backpack just a little, cleared her throat, sniffled, and turned her moist eyes toward Isobel.

"I think it's not knowing what's happening to Matt and not being there with him. We have been through so much together lately, and I have always been right beside him. Right where I belonged and where I wanted to be. No matter what. But not this time. And I can't help but believe he needs me more than ever right now. Matt is a very strong man with deep convictions, and I know he will stand up to whatever is thrown at him. But he can't always do this alone, and he needs help from his friends and me sometimes to make it through. But I am not there, and his friends may not be able to help him either. God only knows what is happening to all of them right now."

"Would it help if I could get you an update on how Matt and his friends are doing?"

Kelli stared blankly at Isobel again. "What do you mean? You can do that?"

Isobel just smiled reassuringly and addressed the driver. "Hanson, would you be kind enough to make a call to the senator and check on our friends who are being held at Langley?"

"Certainly, Mrs. Renner."

Hanson touched some controls on the steering wheel and initiated the call. He directed the call through the car's sound system so all could hear. He wanted the Renners to hear exactly what he heard.

A voice came on the line. "Hello, Mr. Hanson. How are my guests doing? You are taking good care of them?"

"Yes, of course I am, Senator Lange. They are safe, and we will be arriving at Coral Creek airport in just a few minutes."

"Good, Mr. Hanson. Have you determined whether you truly are Isobel's favorite after all?" the senator asked.

"She insists that I am, and I choose to take her at her word," Hanson replied with a slight smile on his face. "You are on car speaker, Senator. Mrs. Renner has made a request."

"I see. What can I do for Isobel?" the senator asked.

"For Kelli Renner's peace of mind, Isobel would like an update on our friends at Langley."

"I do not want Kelli to be distraught over this whole thing," the senator replied. "I have been receiving updates continually, and I assure you that the only abuse the three of them have suffered so far is being bored to death with empty threats and questions they cannot answer, as well as being served institutional food. I can't say the same for Mr. Dominion and the terrorists. They have not had it so easy. Will you take my word on this, Kelli?"

"First of all, thank you for all you are doing for us, Senator Lange. I don't know you personally, but if you are a true friend of Isobel's, then I can only assume you are telling me the truth."

The senator chuckled on the line and responded, "Kelli, Isobel and I go back a long way, and I would do anything for her that is in my power to do. And this is in my power to do. Please believe that I have the situation under constant surveillance and will not let harm come to any of those three fine men who are being held, or to you and your grandmother."

Isobel piped in. "Hey! You best be careful, Carter Lange, with those 'grandmother' references."

A robust laugh erupted from the car speakers.

"I know how much you hate that, Isobel. Just trying to lighten the mood a little," the senator said. "Kelli, please try not to worry. There are lots of people watching this situation right now, and I believe it will all turn out fine in the end."

"Thank you again, Senator. You are being so kind. I can't tell you how much this means to me," Kelli said.

"My pleasure, Kelli. Now, if you will excuse me, I have a meeting to attend. My housekeeping staff have prepared rooms for both of you, and I will be with you for dinner tonight. See you soon."

The line disconnected, and Hanson ended the call using his steering wheel controls.

"Is that satisfactory, Mrs. Renner?" Hanson inquired while looking at Isobel in the rearview mirror.

"Yes, that was perfect, Hanson. You really *are* my favorite, you know."

CHAPTER 56

CIA Holding Cell
Langley, Virginia

Jake paced back and forth in the tiny holding cell he had been banished to. Gray walls. Gray concrete floors. No windows. Tiny cot in one corner. Stainless steel toilet and washbasin in the other. A small light in the ceiling covered with steel mesh to keep the cell's occupant from smashing it. A camera positioned in the back corner to allow for constant observation.

The gray room matched Jake's cloudy disposition. He had done a lot of thinking while stuck in this cell with nothing else to do.

Is this the sum total of my life? Is this how I'm to be rewarded for serving my country without a thought for myself or my own safety for all those years? What am I guilty of? I helped a friend stay alive. That's all. So much for "serving a grateful nation."

So, is this how it ends? I survive all those firefights and missions only to be taken down by those I have been loyal to? Threatened with the loss of my freedom and everything I have worked for?

Jake kicked the small gray bed out of frustration, but it didn't give. It was bolted to the gray floor. And, he hurt his big toe. Dejected, angry, and frustrated, he sat on the side of the cot and put his head in his hands.

I have no family to wonder where I am or what is happening to me. I know that Matt and Kelli and Ghost will be worrying about me, but that isn't the same *as an actual family. My parents dying in that house fire when I was just a kid made me a perfect CIA recruiting target while still in college. Seemed like a good idea to me at the time. They like to recruit people with nothing to lose.*

I've only had fleeting glimpses of the love of a woman. Kicked all those kind souls to the curb as well. All in service to my country, I told myself. Didn't have time to spend with anyone for long. There were women who were willing to deal with my being gone all the time and leaving on short notice, but it wouldn't have been fair to any of them. Now that I have finally retired and could have considered a serious relationship with a woman, I am so screwed up, so damaged, and so full of death and violence, I could not ask anyone else to live with it like I have to. At least I had my marina and some good friends. But now, they want to take that last piece of my life away, too.

Jake glared up at the camera in the high corner of his cell and gave it a vigorous middle finger salute.

CHAPTER 57

Coral Creek Airport
Near Boca Grande, Florida

HANSON SWUNG THE LONG, sleek limousine off Placida Road and through the gates of Coral Creek Airport. It was a small, out-of-the-way jetport that could still handle good-sized private aircraft without the hassle and prying eyes of a larger facility. It also served its share of wealthy and celebrity clients who flew in to vacation in nearby Boca Grande. In the interest of staying off the radar, so to speak, Coral Creek had been the best option.

Hanson slowly approached the largest and most beautiful aircraft in sight. He pulled up to the fully extended boarding stairs and stopped the car. He stepped out of the car and opened both rear passenger doors for Isobel and Kelli. Hanson then opened the trunk and extracted their travel bags. One of the two pilots of the gleaming jet hurried down the steps and assisted Hanson with carrying the luggage over to the external cargo compartment and making sure they were secure before locking the cargo hold door. The other pilot was busy going through his pre-flight checklist and starting the engines.

Before mounting the stairs leading into the sleek, navy blue, white, and gold jet, Isobel turned to Hanson and gave him a robust hug and a warm kiss on the cheek.

"Until next time?" she said.

"Until next time," Hanson replied with a wide smile.

With that, Isobel and Kelli climbed the boarding stairs and entered the luxurious main cabin of the upscale aircraft. The captain and co-pilot emerged from the flight deck and approached them as they were settling in. Isobel looked up at the captain with an inquiring look.

"Good afternoon, Captain. I don't believe we have met."

"You are correct, Mrs. Renner. I have not had the pleasure of being your pilot until now. My name is Captain Jessup, and your co-pilot today is Captain Didier. I believe you have flown with him before."

"Yes, I have. Good to see you again, Captain Didier. I would like for both of you to meet my lovely, uh … associate, Kelli."

Kelli held out her hand to the pilots and commented with a wry tone of voice, "Good to meet you, gentlemen. I am Isobel's granddaughter to be accurate. She has an issue with the whole grandmother thing."

"We will be careful with our language then, Mrs. Renner," Captain Jessup said with a sizable grin.

Quickly changing the subject, Isobel asked a question. "Captain Jessup, I have not flown in this plane before. What is this gorgeous aircraft?"

"She is a Gulfstream G650. Top of the line in the private jet world. Has a range of over 7500 nautical miles and can exceed 600 mph. It normally seats up to fourteen passengers, but as you can see, it has been configured for fewer people with more amenities."

Isobel took in the glove leather lounges and chairs, the kitchen and restroom facilities in the rear, the polished wood trim, and the full bar in the front right corner. The posh interior enveloped them with stripes and splashes of cream, white, and burgundy. Mirrors were tastefully placed at intervals around the cabin, giving it an appearance of being larger than it was.

"I am impressed, Captain Jessup. This is a beautiful aircraft. How much would it set me back if I wanted to purchase one?"

Jessup smiled and replied, "The old saying is that if you have to ask how much it costs, you can't afford it and, in this case, that may be true. This jet, as is, would cost about sixty-four million dollars."

Isobel let out a low whistle and digested that piece of information.

"And who might be the owner of this fine plane? This is not one of those typical white, stripped-down government Learjets."

"Actually, Mrs. Renner, I don't know who owns it. I just show up and fly it when called. Then payments show up in my bank account."

"Hmmm … I'm not sure even my friend Senator Lange can afford to own one of these."

"Hard to say, Mrs. Renner. If you will excuse us, you are expected in Virginia soon. It will take a few minutes to button up and finish the pre-flight checks, so feel free to fix yourself drinks from the bar or some snacks from the pantry. I will signal back when you have to buckle in for takeoff."

Isobel wasted no time in raiding the bar and discovering a nice bottle of chilled Pinot Noir, which she opened and poured liberally into two sizable wine glasses. She sat down on a beige-colored leather lounge next to Kelli, handed her one of the glasses, and raised hers in a toast.

"To the future," Isobel said.

Kelli clinked wine glasses with Isobel but wondered just what "future" she was facing.

The "fasten seatbelt" sign flashed on, and the Renner women buckled in and prepared for takeoff.

One glass of wine might not be enough Kelli decided as she felt the sleek jet start to slowly roll down the runway toward an unknown destination … and destiny.

CHAPTER 58

NASA Administration Building
Kennedy Space Center
Florida

"KEN, THIS IS JOSEPH. I've not heard a word from Matt in days. Do you know what's going on? I thought that they were all back home here in Florida and letting things calm down for a while."

"Well, that was their plan, but unfortunately, it's not that simple anymore," Ken said.

"What do you mean?" Joseph asked.

"I was getting ready to call and tell you. I just found out through an old friend who works in the intel section at the CIA that they have rounded up Matt, Ghost, and Jake and taken them to Langley for interrogation."

"Are you frickin' kidding me?" Joseph replied. "The CIA? What the hell do they have to do with this?"

"As you know, Jake and Ghost are both ex-CIA operatives. When Matt needed help getting safely off Bimini and back to the mainland, he allowed Jake to call in some favors from his friends at the Shop. As you can imagine, this brought them into the loop on the whole thing, and they want answers. They also have Dominion and some of his operatives in custody and have learned enough about the relics and their potential value that they want to take possession of them as a matter of national security."

"Wait, Ken, you said they have Matt, Ghost, and Jake. Where's Kelli?"

"They don't have her, Joseph."

"How can that be?"

"They can't find her evidently. My guess is that Matt gave her the relics and sent her off to hide out somewhere. But I can't imagine where she could hide that the CIA wouldn't have found her by now. However, my source says she has not been located even though there is a huge manhunt for her. Her grandmother Isobel has disappeared along with her."

"This thing has spun out of control! I don't know how to help Matt. NASA has very little influence over those pompous mad dogs at the CIA. What can we do? Carol is worried sick about all this."

"I don't know. Cindy is driving me nuts, wanting answers, too. Speaking of Carol, did you ever find out how she got out of that house where she was being held by the kidnappers?"

"Not a clue. Damned big mystery to everyone who was involved. I'm just glad she was rescued by that mystery angel, whoever it was. Scariest night of my life."

"Yeah, that is a strange one for sure. Well, duty calls. I've got a staff meeting getting ready to start here at the Station. I will let you know anything I know as soon as I get it. I'm sure Matt or Kelli or someone will surface at some point and get a message to us about what is going on."

"Please do. Thank you."

CHAPTER 59

Agent John Milburn's Office
CIA Headquarters
Langley, Virginia

JOHN MILBURN STARED AT the phone on his credenza as if it were a deadly pit viper waiting to bite him if he dared reach out to touch it. He knew the deputy director of the CIA was waiting on his report, but he had nothing new to offer concerning the whereabouts of Kelli Renner and the relics. Or her grandmother. The director was not going to be pleased.

This day had already been a hard one to stomach with having to interrogate Matt, Jake, and Ghost. A task he had not relished but one he did not want to hand off to people who didn't appreciate them for the decent people they are. Add that to the frustration of not being able to get any kind of lead on Kelli and Isobel Renner. Agent Milburn was nearing his wit's end. Now, it was time to face even more unpleasant music from his boss.

"Please put me through to the deputy director on a secure line."

Music on hold.

"Milburn, tell me you have something worthwhile to report this time?"

"Sorry to say, sir, but the situation has not changed since we last spoke."

"You can't be serious. Nothing new at all?"

"No, sir. We have serious resources working on every front. Credit card transactions, phone records, airline reservations, police reports, accident and hospital reports, or anything else that might disclose their location or what has happened to them."

"Then there is only one explanation for such a complete vanishing act. Someone is helping them."

"We have found nothing in their past histories or in recent events to indicate any foreign alliance or group affiliation. If anything, they have exhibited a life-long pattern of strong independence."

"How else would you explain this ability to disappear into thin air and avoid the most advanced intelligence gathering apparatus the world has ever known?"

John Milburn felt his blood rising and his face flushing. He was nearing his breaking point. "For God's sake, Director, I can't explain it, and neither can anyone else. We are doing everything we know to do at this point, but it is not helpful to put your foot up my ass every couple hours!"

Milburn could see his career going up in flames even as he spoke. *But by God, enough is enough!*

There was a long pause on the line before the director spoke again.

"I probably deserve that. Point taken. The pressure is immense from the top down to find those relics before someone else does. One of the reasons I made you the point man on this mission is because you are one of the best the Agency has to offer. The other reason is because of your personal relationship with Jake. I thought that might work to our benefit, but looking at it now, I can see where I put you and Ghost's handler both in a tough position. I know you say that all three of them claim they have no knowledge of where the Renners and the relics might be, but do you believe them? You know that Jake and Ghost are trained in deception. Perhaps Matt is too when you consider his service in Naval Intelligence."

"I appreciate you not burning me to the ground, Director. I know I was insubordinate, but this has been a bitch—excuse my language. In all honesty, I would have to say that I believe them all at this point. We ran polygraphs, speech analysis, facial pattern recognition. You name it, we did it. No deception was indicated from any of them. My best guess is that Matt was truthful when he said he sent

Kelli to her grandmother's house to buy time, and he doesn't know anything beyond that. We had his cell phone, so we know he didn't receive any communications from the Renners. That would certainly exonerate Jake and Ghost as they were in custody and already out of the loop by then."

"Understood, and I tend to agree with your analysis, but we can't allow this situation to stand the way it is. As much as it runs against your grain, I want you to hold them in custody here until something breaks. Since the Renners know those three are in our custody, they might eventually come to us voluntarily to try to have them exonerated and freed. That is about the only leverage we have left at this time."

"We will remain vigilant and continue the search by all means available to us, but it might be time to let the game come to us."

"Agreed. Keep up the good work and keep me informed of any and all developments."

"Count on it, Director."

"I am."

CHAPTER 60

Andrews Air Force Base
Joint Base Andrews
Prince Georges County, Maryland

THE GLEAMING GULFSTREAM JET taxied down the runway at Joint Base Andrews in Prince Georges County, Maryland, the base where Air Force One is hangared, along with many other government agency planes. The Gulfstream rolled unimpeded to a private hangar area where no customs officials were required or allowed. It had special security clearances across the board. As soon as it rolled to a stop, an unmarked black SUV approached at high speed and waited for the stairway to be let down by the flight crew.

Once the stairway was fully extended and secured, the driver of the SUV emerged to collect the passengers. As had been the case with Hanson, the young man appeared to be military by his cut and demeanor. He was also attired in a black, tailored business suit with a black tie and white shirt. His dress shoes were polished to a high gloss, and his hair was cut high and tight.

Isobel and Kelli exited the plane, pausing to thank both pilots for their hospitality and a smooth flight. As they descended the stairway, they noticed their new driver/valet/bodyguard, and who knows what else. Of course, Isobel engaged him immediately.

"Well, hello young man! I do not believe I have had the pleasure of meeting you before. Are you new to this detail?"

"Yes, ma'am. The senator requested my services a couple of weeks ago."

"Then, you must have an exemplary record if you were requested by the senator?"

"I do my best, ma'am."

"I'm sure you do. Do you have a name?"

"My name is Daniels, ma'am."

"Well, Daniels, it's good to meet you. My name is Isobel, by the way. No 'ma'am' if you please. And, this is my associate, Kelli."

Daniels shook both their hands very quickly and formally. Kelli rolled her eyes at her grandmother's use of 'associate' again. She let it pass this time.

"Now, Daniels, you may have heard by now that everyone on the detail wants to be my favorite," Isobel said with a serious look.

"Yes, ma'am—uh, I mean Isobel. I have heard it mentioned, and it seems to be true. Do you currently have a favorite?"

"Of course, dear."

"May I ask who it is, so I know who I have to beat out for the honor?"

"Simple, Mr. Daniels. It is whoever I am with at the moment. So you are now my new favorite!"

Daniels could not fully suppress his laugh though he tried to remain circumspect. He moved to the side of the aircraft where the pilots were offloading the luggage. He picked up the Renners' bags and stowed them inside the back compartment of the spacious SUV. He then moved to the passenger doors, opened them for his guests, shut them once they were inside, and got into the driver's seat where he proceeded to drive away from the airport and toward Virginia.

The drive to the senator's residence in McLean took close to an hour, which allowed time for Kelli to continue her questioning of Isobel.

"Isobel, why can't you tell me what's going on here? Why is a United States senator willing to take us in and protect us from his own government agency? And, what is your connection to Senator Lange, by the way?"

"All good questions, my dear, and all will be answered in due time. We will have ample opportunity to discuss this once we are settled in at Carter's home. You will love his family, and they are great hosts."

"My God, I hope we are not jumping from the frying pan right into the fire!"

Isobel turned toward her and looked Kelli directly in the eyes with a look of both firmness and compassion.

"My dear, there are many things that have gone on and are still going on in this world that are unknown to you … and for that matter … unknown to almost everyone on this planet. You will have to trust me when I tell you there are forces at play that do not answer to this government, or any other. There is a bigger picture to be seen here, and you will be given the opportunity to understand your part in that picture very soon. So, try to remain patient for just a little longer. I only ask that you treat our hosts with the respect they deserve and let things proceed at a comfortable pace for all concerned. Can you do that much for me?"

Kelli peered back at Isobel with a look of exasperation and resignation. "I guess I'll have to. I know we owe the senator a large debt of gratitude, and I will be sure to let him know how much I appreciate his generosity and kindness."

Isobel smiled warmly at her granddaughter of whom she was so proud, then kissed the tip of her finger and placed it on Kelli's lips as a sign of her deep affection. Kelli returned the gesture.

The ride continued in silence as Kelli's thoughts returned to Matt.

I wonder how Matt is doing right now? He has no idea where I am or what is going on, and I don't know how to get a message to him. He must be going crazy worrying about me and the artifacts. God, I miss him so much. I have to find a way to communicate with him.

CHAPTER 61

Senator Carter Lange's Residence
McLean, Virginia

THE LONG, BLACK SUV entered the senator's residence through a remote-controlled pair of white wrought-iron security gates with surveillance cameras mounted one on each side. As Daniels cleared the gates, he proceeded slowly up the long, tree-lined lane past manicured hedgerows and white iron lamp posts. The driveway eventually opened into a full circle directly in front of a breathtaking manor house. The driver pulled around the circle and stopped in front of the covered portico leading to the home's main entrance.

Daniels exited the car and opened the doors for Isobel and Kelli. As they stepped out, he moved to the back of the vehicle to retrieve their luggage. Isobel had started walking toward the house's massive front doors when she realized Kelli was not beside her. She stopped and looked back to find Kelli still standing beside the SUV. Isobel chuckled under her breath and went back to get her.

"Isobel, I have never seen a house like this in my life! Your house is to die for, but this is like something out of a movie," Kelli said.

"Yes, it is quite an astounding sight the first time you see it. Carter will be too modest to brag about it, so I'll tell you a few things about it that I have learned. It's over twenty thousand square feet and sits on seven acres. There are eight bedrooms and eleven bathrooms, including two master suites. The exterior is Italian limestone and marble. There is a library made entirely of mahogany, a cinema, billiards room, cigar room, wine cellar, music room, twelve-person spa, and an infinity pool out back. Now, close your mouth and put your eyes back in your head, and let's go meet your hosts."

Isobel pulled Kelli up the steps to the main doors and rang the doorbell while Daniels brought up the rear with their bags. Within seconds, the tall, stately doors swung open, and a strikingly beautiful woman stood smiling with her arms outstretched.

"Isobel! How are you? Please come in and give me a hug!"

"Oh, my goodness, Stephanie. You look better every time I see you! I'm doing very well, thank you. It's so wonderful to see you again."

The two old friends embraced warmly before Isobel pulled away and took the arm of her granddaughter and pulled her forward.

"Stephanie, this is Kelli."

Stephanie wrapped Kelli in a warm embrace, then stood back a step while keeping her hand on Kelli's shoulders, and said, "Oh my God, it's been years since I saw you last. You were just a little girl when we would occasionally see you at your grandmother's … uh … Isobel's home!"

The faux pas elicited a belly laugh from everyone, and Kelli felt more at ease.

"You have grown into a beautiful woman, Kelli," Stephanie offered.

"Thank you, Mrs. Lange, but I'm sure I look pretty rough at the moment. It's been a crazy few days. Crazy few weeks, actually."

"So I have heard. Carter has told me a little of the story. We are all family here, so you must call me Stephanie."

"Speaking of family, where is Carter?" Isobel inquired.

"He is finishing up his business in D. C. and will be headed home soon," Stephanie replied. "In the meantime, I will fix us a before-dinner cocktail, give you a quick tour of the house so Kelli will feel more at home, and get you settled into your rooms so you can freshen up before dinner. Carter should be home in time to join us for the evening meal."

CHAPTER 62

Earth Defense Force
Rapid Response Team Staging Area
Near McLean, Virginia

"LISTEN UP, PEOPLE! WE are sixty minutes to go time. I know that some of you think this is going to be a piece of cake. Tactically, it may look that way. But, as you all know too well, every mission faces the unexpected at some point."

"Though this is a relatively soft target compared to many we have encountered in the past, it has strategic importance beyond anything you can imagine. Therefore, we must execute with precision and speed. No mistakes. Understood?"

"Yes, sir!" came the reply from the ten men assembled in the empty warehouse.

"Good! We expect minimal resistance, and the extraction should be completed within ten minutes after engagement of our targets. Is everyone clear on the objectives and your role in the mission? I want each of you to tell me what your role is during this deployment."

One by one, the black-clad warriors in the room took turns reciting in detail to the commander precisely what their job would be in the upcoming mission as well as the overall objective.

"Well done, men. You are the best of the best. That's why you are here today. Any questions?"

One of the ten spoke up. "Commander, could you clarify the rules of engagement, including the use of deadly force?"

"I will make this as simple as I can, so there is no misunderstanding. We are to use no more force than necessary to reach our strategic goals, but we are to use *all* force necessary should the mission require it. Failure is not an option here, gentlemen. This mission could very well determine the future and security of our planet and those who call it home. Is that a big enough reason for you guys to get ramped up? Now, ready yourselves for departure."

CHAPTER 63

CIA Headquarters
Langley, Virginia

THE PHONE ON JOHN Milburn's desk buzzed. It was his receptionist. He reached over and pressed the button on the intercom. "Yes, Sylvia."

"The director is on the secure line."

"Okay, thanks."

Damn it, now what?

Milburn took a deep breath, calmed himself, and poked the blinking button for the secure line.

"Good afternoon, Director."

"John, I want to speak with you about the status of our three detainees."

"They are still in solitary confinement."

"Yes, I know that. But after giving it a lot of thought, I have concluded that this wait-and-see game of using them as leverage is not going to be the best way to go. It's moving too slow, and I'm not convinced that it will get the results we want. The longer this plays out, the less chance we have of finding a warm trail to those artifacts."

"Understood, sir, and I have come to the same conclusion. What are you thinking?"

"Release them. Then, watch their every move. Tag their phones, shoes, clothes, or any other personal belongings that will be returned to them. Then track them every second after their release. Eventually,

I believe there will be contact between Matt and Kelli Renner. I feel confident about that. I think it best to let the foxes run and find out where the den is. Agreed?"

"Agreed, sir. Jake always says playing offense is better than being on the defensive, so I expect he will find a way to go back on offense in this scenario. I believe this approach has a better chance of producing something tangible."

"Very well, Milburn. I'm glad we're on the same page with this thing. See to it that the three of them are released quickly … after you organize surveillance and fast response teams, of course."

"Consider it done, Director. I will keep you updated on their movements and any intel we gather."

"Good. Don't make me call and ask."

CHAPTER 64

UNITED STATES SENATOR CARTER Lange raised his wine glass and proposed a toast.

As all raised their glasses, he said, "To old friends and new memories!"

Everyone who was seated around the large, ornate dining room table, responded by clinking their wine glasses with the persons seated next to them, taking a sip, and sharing warm smiles.

"Isobel, this is an excellent wine you selected from the cellar. Have you had it before?"

"Thank you, Carter, but I don't think I have."

"Then what made you choose it, may I ask?"

"Well, it was all a very scientific process as you might expect. If you look at the label, it says it originated at Lady Isobel Vineyards in Spain. So, I decided it had to be an excellent wine!"

Bright laughter rippled around the table as dishes of pasta, meats and sauces, and warm bread were passed around. The merry clatter of utensils and china serving dishes and plates made for a pleasant backdrop to the gathering.

Kelli stood, cleared her throat, and held up her wine glass. "Senator, with your permission, I would like to make a toast as well."

Senator Lange said, "Please do so, my dear."

Kelli looked intently at each friendly face at the table. Isobel, the senator, Stephanie, and Autumn, the senator's young daughter.

"I don't mean to put a damper on things, but I want to offer a toast to three very important people who cannot be with us tonight—Matt, Jake, and Ghost."

Everyone nodded, clinked glasses, and took a solemn sip.

Senator Lange said, "Believe me, Kelli, I am watching the situation closely and will let you know of any changes as they occur."

"I know you will, and that is a great comfort to me, Senator. It's so hard for me to relax and enjoy myself while they're still at risk."

"Perfectly understandable, Kelli. It's alright. We will continue to do all we can."

Kelli sat back down, took another drink of wine, and picked at her plate of food.

CHAPTER 65

SPECIAL AGENT MILBURN SAT quietly behind his desk as one by one, Matt, Jake, and Ghost were brought in with their hands cuffed behind their backs and legs shackled to the point of allowing only enough freedom to take small, shuffling steps. He directed the security personnel to seat them at his conference table.

"Un-cuff them," Milburn ordered.

The security officers paused and looked at him. It was obvious they were uncomfortable with this new order. They had been forewarned of the prisoners' capabilities.

"Legs and hands both, sir?"

"Yes, take all the cuffs off, dammit!"

The officers quickly moved to unlock and remove all the restraints, then stood up with their hands resting on their sidearms just in case the prisoners tried something.

"No need for that, guys. You can stand down now. I'll take it from here. Thank you and you're dismissed."

The guards glanced warily at each other, looked nervously at Agent Milburn, but shuffled on out of the room.

The three unwilling guests of Hotel Langley were now staring intently at John Milburn, wondering what was going to happen next.

"How you guys doin'? Enjoying your stay with us so far?" Milburn asked innocently as if he were a customer service agent at a resort hotel. It was not well received.

"What the hell is going on here?" Matt growled with barely controlled rage in his voice.

Milburn seemed unfazed by Matt's reaction and continued in a lighthearted tone. "Well, it seems to be your lucky day, gentlemen. As of this moment, you are all free to go."

After a stunned silence, Jake spoke next. "Why would our wonderful hosts suddenly decide just to turn us loose?"

"Don't look a gift horse in the mouth, Jake."

"John, I know this horse too damned well. There's a catch to this and something they hope to gain by letting us go."

"Nope. No conditions. You've been released."

"Is this because you have already found Kelli?" Matt said.

"No, we don't know where she is yet. The director just doesn't feel there are adequate legal grounds to hold the three of you any longer."

"Bullshit, John!" Ghost replied. "You guys had all these different crimes you were going to charge us with and could have made most of them stick more than likely."

"Well Ghost, that's true. But the director is in a forgiving mood with you and Jake being part of the family and all."

Jake laughed out loud at that statement and said, "The only reason we would be released at this point is that the director has decided we are more valuable on the street than in a cell. Problem is, we have no idea where Kelli or the relics are, and you know it."

Milburn sat quietly for a few moments staring at Jake and tapping his fingers on the metal table.

"Whatever the case may be, Jake, you three are free to go. All personal belongings you had when you arrived will be brought to you shortly. Security will escort you out. And for whatever it's worth guys … I really am sorry this happened."

With that, John Milburn stood up and left the room while talking to himself in his head … *sometimes I really hate the shit I have to do in this job.*

CHAPTER 66

Earth Defense Force
Staging Area
Near McLean, Virginia

"Time to saddle up, boys. Check your weapons and equipment one last time and prepare to move out," the commander barked.

Weapons clicking and bags being zipped and unzipped were the only sounds to be heard. The men were silent and focused as they went through their final checks.

The double doors to the warehouse opened wide, and two small white box trucks pulled through the doors and into the interior of the building. They were painted with a fictitious home security company logo and identification on both sides. The drivers, who were dressed in regular work clothes with the fake company logo on them as well, got out of the truck and walked to the rear where they unlocked and pushed up the rear cargo doors of the trucks.

The ten members of the recon team stood and walked to the rear of the trucks, five to each truck plus the commander, who would ride in the lead truck. The commander looked inside each of the trucks before allowing his men to load in. The trucks were bare inside other than metal benches running down each side of the interior, cargo netting on the walls, and a LED light strip running down the center of the ceiling.

The commander satisfied himself that everything looked as it should and waved his men into the trucks.

"Alright, you badasses, let's go save the world today. Mount up!" the commander shouted as he stepped up into the truck, watched his men load in, and lowered the rear door.

He then clicked on his comm device and told the drivers, "Let's roll!"

CHAPTER 67

CIA Headquarters
Langley, Virginia

THREE SECURITY PERSONNEL ESCORTED Matt, Jake, and Ghost from the deep interior of the large intelligence complex to the front entrance lobby. It was approaching winter, and they had put on the heavy jackets they had brought with them when forced to leave Florida. Two of the security men turned to walk away, but the third security guard paused long enough to shake their hands. As he shook Matt's hand, a tiny piece of folded paper passed from his hand to Matt's.

"Thank you for your service, gentlemen," he said with a slight smile.

Matt nodded and smiled and had the presence of mind to quickly palm the note and put his hand in his jacket pocket.

The three former captives quickly exited through the main security gate and walked down the street far enough to be away from the watchful eye of the Agency. They ducked into a coffee shop and grabbed a corner table where they could see anyone that might come in through the front door.

"Hey, guys, one of the security guards who escorted us out slipped me a piece of paper," Matt said as he fished the folded piece of paper out of his jacket pocket and started reading it.

"Well, what does it say?" Jake asked impatiently.

Matt chewed on the left corner of his lower lip and replied, "It's an address."

"Where is the address?" Ghost asked.

"It's in McLean, Virginia," Matt answered.

The waitress came over to take their order, and they asked for three black, strong coffees to go.

Jake pulled out his cell phone the Agency had so kindly returned to him, opened his maps app, and punched in the address.

Matt quickly grabbed Jake's hand once he saw what he was doing.

"Jake, why the hell are you doing that? You know they have our cell phones, and God knows what else under surveillance."

"Yeah, I know, but if this is where Kelli is hiding out, we need to find it and get there as soon as possible. We don't have the luxury of wasting time and being careful at this point. We have no idea what has happened or what is going on. We can adjust our plans once we know the situation."

Matt removed his hand from Jake's. "You're probably right, as usual. How far is it to that address?"

Jake made a low whistling sound and showed Matt and Ghost a picture of the property at the address his phone was displaying.

"It looks like Kelli and her grandmother picked a damned nice safe house!" Ghost commented.

"I'm not sure they picked it, but yeah, that's quite a place," Matt said. "I wonder who owns it?"

"We'll find out when we get there. It's about an hour away from here by car," Jake noted.

The waitress showed up with their coffees to go, and Jake pulled out his wallet to pay. He quickly looked through his wallet and discovered that his credit cards and cash were still inside. Matt was about out of financial resources at this point, and Jake knew it. So Jake had decided to bring lots of extra cash and his own credit cards on the trip.

"Well, at least we don't have to add 'thieves' to all the pet names I have for those bastards at the Shop," Jake quipped.

Jake paid for the coffees, and the three of them hurried out into the street and hailed the first taxi that came by.

The taxi driver was a young, long-haired man appearing to be in his late twenties and an accent that sounded faintly Midwestern. Matt told the driver where they wanted to go, and the driver broke into a toothy grin and said, "That's the high rent district over there.

It's a pretty long ride to that part of town, and it will cost you some money. Are you sure about this?"

"Yes, we're sure," Jake replied impatiently. "This is an emergency. If you can get us there in under an hour, there's an extra twenty bucks in it for you. If you don't think you can do that, then I will be glad to take the wheel. So, are you the man for the job?"

The driver laughed out loud as if reveling in the challenge and said, "Strap in dudes and hang on. I never leave money on the table!"

CHAPTER 68

Senator Lange's Residence
McLean, Virginia

Everyone had finished their meals and were watching as Stephanie began preparing after dinner drinks consisting of gourmet coffee with a splash of Bailey's Cream. Senator Lange stood and asked everyone to join him in the sitting room by the fireplace as he had something special to share with them.

The diners collected their ornate china cups and saucers and moved to the sitting room as requested. As they entered the large room, they discovered there were several people already seated there.

Senator Lange moved to greet his new guests and embraced each of them warmly and with affection.

"Please, Kelli, let me introduce you to some of my dearest friends," the senator said. "Isobel and my family are also friends with them, and I am so pleased you now get to meet them as well. These people hold a special place in our lives, and now I believe they will in yours. In fact, I am sure of it."

Kelli looked curiously at these new faces. There were three of them in all, two men and a woman. Kelli stood very still as she remained unsure what was expected of her or what was to unfold during this gathering. The senator smiled and stepped toward her, taking her hand and leading her to an older but handsome man who was standing closest to them. He had sandy blond hair mixed with wisps of white and sparkling gray eyes that seemed to dance in the room's ambient light. He was well dressed in a navy blazer, gray slacks, and a crisp white open-collar shirt. He was fairly tall and trim in build.

"Kelli, I am pleased to introduce you to a longtime friend and associate of mine, Hans Eriksson."

Kelli offered her hand and shook that of Mr. Eriksson's while they exchanged greetings and smiles.

Moving to the next nearest person, the senator said, "Now, I want you to meet my chief legislative aide and another longtime friend, Phil Meade."

Kelli surmised Mr. Meade to be in his late forties, balding with a patch of salt and pepper hair remaining mostly on the sides, and a little bit of a paunch around the middle. He, too, was dressed in a gray sports jacket, navy slacks, and a light blue button-down shirt. After they had shaken hands and exchanged pleasantries, it was time for mystery guest number three.

"Last but not least, Kelli, please meet someone very dear to my heart, Ms. Lindsay Berglund. Lindsay works closely with Hans and is a woman of many talents."

Kelli smiled, took Lindsay's hand, and continued to hold her hand while they locked eyes. Lindsay was a striking woman with long raven-black hair, tall by a woman's standards, porcelain skin. She looked to be in exceptional physical condition as the burgundy sweater dress she wore outlined her figure nicely without being too revealing. Probably in her late thirties or early forties, Kelli thought. But, the most striking thing about her, in Kelli's quickly forming opinion, was her breathtaking emerald green eyes that were wide and almond-shaped. The thought occurred to Kelli that people could get lost in those eyes.

Suddenly, something else caught Kelli's attention. Now, as she held onto Lindsay's hand and looked into the deep, warm pools of her eyes, a strange sensation of warmth emanated from their joined hands. But there was also something else. Something hard to describe or put your finger on. Something playing softly on the outskirts of Kelli's mind. Almost like a feeling of invitation and acceptance. Not alarming, but noticeable. Strange.

Kelli let go of Lindsay's hand, and the unusual sensations faded quickly. Lindsay's face reflected only pure innocence and kindness. Kelli already missed the connection she had briefly experienced. It was comforting, like a warm blanket.

"Please, let us all sit and get to know each other better," Senator Lange said as he gestured around at the empty armchairs and sofas. Once seated, the senator continued the conversation.

"Kelli, I have asked our friends here tonight to assist you in a journey of discovery that will have life-changing ramifications for you, just as they have for me and your grand … uh … Isobel." Poorly hidden smiles flickered at the corners of the mouths of all who were gathered. Isobel's disdain for elderly titles was well known to everyone in her circle of friendship.

The senator continued. "These kind people whom you have just met and their associates and connections throughout the world have assisted me in helping you up to this point. Hans, Phil, and Lindsay are the ones who have been able to gather the information you desired about the status of your friends that were being held. This is but one of the countless times they have worked with me on things we all deem important."

"Who might be the proud owner of that Gulfstream we were fortunate enough to travel here on, might I ask?" Isobel interjected.

"That was also courtesy of Hans and his friends," Senator Lange answered.

"Very impressive. We appreciate all you have done for us."

"Honored to be of assistance, Isobel," Hans replied. "But do not get the wrong impression about my personal wealth, I don't own it alone. It is joint property of myself and many other associates. We travel a lot in our different projects, and it is a way of easing the weariness that comes from it."

"Speaking of projects, I think it is an opportune time to discuss what some these projects are that we have all worked on together and how it pertains to you and your relics, Kelli," Senator Lange said.

CHAPTER 69

THE TWO UNREMARKABLE SECURITY company work trucks slowly coasted to a stop about a block away from the senator's residence. They parked one behind the other and turned off their engines. The rear cargo doors quickly slid up, and the commando team from the Earth Defense Force moved out of the cargo area in a businesslike manner, trying not to arouse suspicion from any nosy neighbors who might be watching. Weapons and tactical gear were well hidden under their winter coats. The mission commander stood by and observed his men as they prepared to launch perhaps their most important deployment ever.

The Earth Defense Force (EDF) had been formed years earlier by a group of well-intentioned patriots who were very highly placed in the military-industrial-intelligence complex of the United States. They had found like-minded allies in the top-secret ranks of officers and politicians of other countries as well. Men and women who shared their concerns over what had been going on around the world for a long time. Things that were unknown except to a few people at the very top of the most clandestine organizations in each major world government and sometimes … outside of those governments. Things presidents and prime ministers were not always made privy to. Things that could not be trusted to temporary occupants of political offices who came and went like the wind with very little thought of whether they had actually made a difference in the world. Things only those who held the power behind the power of the countries of the world could be trusted with. At least, that had been their thought process since this whole thing had started to take shape back in the 1940s. The time when it was determined there were things to be kept from the public as well as their governments. Things that were dangerous. Things that could create widespread panic and chaos in the world's religious, financial, and cultural orders and institutions. Things that had to be managed and controlled at all costs.

One of the necessary strategies had been to develop EDF quick response teams that could move quickly to anywhere in the world to quell and control a situation that would threaten the status quo and stability of the current world order. Threats could come from within the world's governments—or without—at any moment. They had to be ready to respond to either. The EDF had developed sympathetic contacts from deep within the intelligence community, including a well-placed mole on Senator Lange's staff. This is how they had gotten wind of the Atlantis tech discovery and where the current whereabouts of the relics might be.

Now, they had to act swiftly for two primary reasons.

One, to make sure this revolutionary technology did not fall into anyone else's hands, including the military and intelligence establishments of the United States. None of them could be trusted with the knowledge that might be revealed by this discovery.

Second, this technology could be the break they had been waiting for. It could provide the means by which Earth could finally develop weapons and space technology that would enable it to defend itself against external invaders and the unwelcome visitations that had persisted throughout mankind's history.

The commander gave the order to move out. The first team of five operatives walked nonchalantly down the street and then suddenly disappeared into hedges and tree lines and out of view of other houses. Their job was to surround the perimeter of the senator's house and make sure no one got in or out while the operation was underway.

The second team was tasked with carrying out the actual extraction of the artifacts. Piercing the outer security layers would be relatively easy, but once inside, they had no idea of what resistance they might be facing, or the whereabouts of the relics themselves. Time would be a factor, and they had to move decisively and with conviction. Forcibly raiding a sitting senator's residence was not a matter to be undertaken lightly.

Team Two proceeded toward the large iron security gates that protected the senator's mansion. The five team members in their black tactical gear melted quickly into hedgerows while the work-uniformed truck drivers quickly began the process of disabling the surveillance and alarm systems. It would appear they were doing routine maintenance on the gate system to anyone casually passing by.

The drivers had rehearsed this scenario countless times over the last few days and had become proficient to the point of being able to take down a security system identical to the one on these gates in less than a minute. The mansion and its occupants would now be blind to and unwarned of what was taking place just outside.

Team One signaled on the commander's comm unit they were now in place around the home's perimeter.

All five members of Team Two now moved through the security gates and blended into the tree lines and hedgerows as best they could as they made their way up the lane toward the house. They readied their weapons and stun grenades as they moved forward.

They quickly reached their objective and huddled on each side of the massive front doors. From their research of the house plans, they had determined the front doors to be the best way to quickly access the part of the house where they believed the occupants were most likely to be gathered. Speed to the objective was essential. They now readied their plastic explosives to blow the doors if needed.

One of the members of Team Two gingerly tried the doorknobs to the large doors and found them unlocked. Evidently, the senator was very reliant on his gate and perimeter security system. The team huddled into a tightly bunched formation and awaited the signal from the commander, who had now joined them at the door. The commander stood to the side of his operatives, paused to allow them to balance themselves and mentally prepare for this final push, then pumped his left hand in a 'go' sign and yelled, "Move, move, move!"

The skilled fighters quickly opened the big doors and burst through as they had practiced so many times. They swiftly moved deeper into the residence toward voices they could now hear coming from the room beyond the dining room. They continued forward with speed but without rushing, sweeping their lethal weapons from side to side. Team Two paused at the entry to the sitting room where the occupants of the home were gathered. The commander gave the signal to go again, and they stepped through the sitting room doors and spread out into the room. The commander immediately shouted, "DO NOT MOVE!" to the shocked people in front of him. They all froze and complied with the order … except Kelli. This sort of thing had become her new normal, and she would not freeze or panic.

She did not know who they were, but she already knew why they were there and what they were after … and she also realized what she must do next.

Kelli began stepping slowly backward toward a hallway behind her, trying not to draw attention. Unfortunately, she realized, she was the main focus of the intruders' attention as they knew who she was and that she was the quickest route to finding the artifacts.

The commander noticed her movements and quickly ordered her to stop. Kelli hesitated for a moment, then turned and sprinted as fast as she could down the hallway toward her guest bedroom, betting they would not shoot her as long as they did not know the location of what they came for.

The commando who been stationed nearest her broke into quick pursuit and would have overtaken her except for the actions of the senator who had played football in college. Just as the pursuer was about to grab her, Senator Lange launched himself at the soldier's legs and made a tackle that was ugly but effective. The commando rolled over and kicked the senator in the face to free himself, but the senator doggedly grabbed onto his legs again. One of the other operatives then stepped over and used the butt of his assault weapon to hit the senator on the back of the head, leaving him dazed. The commander shouted for them to pursue Kelli and bring her back immediately. The one who had struck the senator had already moved into the hallway giving chase while the other operative was untangling himself from the senator's clutches.

Kelli flew like the wind to her room and retrieved the backpack full of priceless relics from under the bed. Kelli had purposely paid close attention during Stephanie's tour of the house as to where the other exits and entrances were located. She had grown accustomed to thinking strategically over the last few weeks and Jake had taught them many things from his bag of tricks. She quickly worked her way through a maze of hallways and rooms until she was approaching the back door leading out into the back yard and pool area.

Just as she was reaching for the handle to the back door, she heard a strong male voice tell her to stop and not move. Stopping no longer seemed to be an option to Kelli after all this. She would not … could not … just surrender and give up after all the sacrifice and loss. Matt wouldn't. Neither would she. She turned to look at her pursuer and could not make out the features of his countenance since he was masked in black. No way to ascertain if mercy lived in his heart or had been trained out of him. The voice now informed her not to move, or he would shoot.

Maybe he would … maybe he wouldn't. She would just have to find out.

Kelli set her jaw, gritted her teeth, and launched herself at the back door, trying to open it and get through it all in the same motion. Luckily, it was not locked, and as she pulled it open, she heard the operative say, "NO!" She took another step toward freedom, someone rushed past her from the outside, and the next thing she heard was the sharp report of the gunman's rifle aimed squarely at her back.

CHAPTER 70

CIA SPECIAL AGENT JOHN Milburn was preparing to address his hastily assembled team of highly trained field agents. Milburn had put together two teams of ten, borrowing any qualified personnel that were available on short notice. He believed that, knowing the skill levels of the people he was going after, it would take at least twenty field operatives to contain this situation they were about to enter into. He wished he had twenty more.

"Listen up! I know you have been brought here on short notice with no idea what you are being asked to do. So, what's new? That's what we signed up for. I will tell you what I can. I cannot possibly bring you up to speed on all the details of why this mission is so important because we have to move out in just a few moments. We are already behind the clock on this one.

"What I will tell you is this. We are tasked with making a forcible entry into a senator's residence in McLean. I am not sure who will be in the residence when we arrive, but there are three individuals you need to be concerned about. One is ex-CIA black ops. Name is Jake. We tapped his cell phone, and that is how we obtained this address we are moving to. Yes, he knows we tapped it, but he is betting he can get there before us and get out.

"The second one is also ex-CIA black ops. Goes by nickname Ghost. Expert in deception and stealth.

"Third one is Matt. Ex-Naval Intelligence. Not as dangerous as the other two, but don't let him get hold of anything to swing at you, like a bat.

"Listen carefully, ladies and gentlemen, I cannot stress to you enough how capable Jake and Ghost are. This mission is to contain them, not kill them. They are heroes in every sense of the word, and they have just been trying to protect their friend Matt from harm. However, this has become a problem for the Agency. Matt is in possession of some very important items that are now classified to be of the greatest importance to our national security. We must secure these items during this mission. No matter what it takes. This may be the most consequential mission any of you will ever take part in. It's that important.

"Again, we will attempt to get them to stand down and do this peacefully. But I don't know how they will react even when faced with overwhelming force. They are trained to beat the odds and have done so many times over. I will go over the mission planning with you on the way. We will chopper over to McLean as it is the only way we will make up enough time to effectively accomplish the mission. We will have an intrusion team of ten with a backup team of ten. We will land the two choppers in a church parking lot about a quarter-mile from the target residence. From there, we will double-time it to our objective. No more force is to be used than necessary. But if necessary, lethal force is authorized. Let's go earn our government pay. Move out!"

CHAPTER 71

D. C. Taxi
Approaching Senator Lange's Residence
McLean, Virginia

"How much longer?" Matt asked the taxi driver.

"We're just a couple of blocks out. It is around the corner of that street up ahead, and about halfway down, I think. At least, that's the way it looks on my GPS."

"And it looks like you made it in about fifty minutes," Jake commented. "Guess you earned your twenty-dollar bonus. You need to let us out right here and then leave the area without delay."

Jake paid the pricey cab fare and pulled an extra twenty out of his wallet as he had promised. The driver flashed his toothy smile again and said he was glad to be of service. He pulled his ball cap low over his eyes and wasted no time in heading back to his normal working area.

Jake, Ghost, and Matt looked around and began to size up their environment. They did not know what they were walking into. Did the CIA goons beat them here? Were Kelli, Isobel, and the artifacts here? Or was it a setup of some kind? They had no weapons other than their hands.

"Matt, I know you are in a real hurry to get in there and see if Kelli is there and if she is okay. I get that. I am too," Jake said. "But we have to do this the smart way if we want to help her. We have to reconnoiter the house before we try to make entry. See what we are walking into or if Kelli and Isobel are even there. You understand?"

"Yeah, I get it. Just give me the plan."

"First thing we should do is check the perimeter for people or things that look out of place. We should do this prior to approaching the house. Once we secure the perimeter, we will look for the best way to gain entry into the house. Probably the back entrance. So, Ghost, I would appreciate it if you would put on your invisibility cloak and check out the perimeter of the property this house sits on. You up for that?"

Ghost smiled his catlike grin … his game face … and replied, "Finally, I get to have some fun." And off he went.

"What now?" Matt inquired.

"As painful as it sounds, we do nothing until Ghost reports back." They chose a particularly large row of hedges grown to act as a privacy fence between mansions and slid into a small opening in the hedgerow to stay out of sight. About ten long, nerve-wracking minutes passed by with no word from Ghost.

"It's been a while, Jake. Do you think something has happened to Ghost?"

Jake glanced at Matt in the dim, gray light of early evening and laid his hand on Matt's shoulder. "I know you are dying to get in that house, but hang in there, Pardner. It will all work out. My thinking is if it has taken this long, Ghost has found something. Poor bastards."

About a minute later, Ghost suddenly appeared, as he often did. He was carrying a duffle bag and a comm unit.

"Brought you guys some souvenirs!" Ghost whispered while opening the duffle bag. Inside the bag were three assault rifles, flash bang grenades, and some combat knives.

"Damn, Ghost! I don't feel so underdressed for this party now that you brought me some new accessories to wear." Jake said. "What in the hell did you find out there?"

"Well, it seems there are some unexpected guests at this event. There were three fully armed operatives hiding out in the back of the property, which means there are probably several more in the front of the house and maybe inside. They had no markings on their tactical gear, so I don't know who they are, but I never did care for uninvited party guests. So, I made them leave the party … sort of. They won't be on the guest list any longer."

"Ghost, you're a dangerous man," Jake chuckled. "I'm sure glad you're on my side. Matt, since Ghost has secured the back side of the house, it would be best to enter through the back door. So, let's see what this party's all about and who's here."

The three men quickly and quietly made their way up the hedgerow and then across a small stretch of open yard to the back of the senator's residence.

"I'm going in first," Jake said in a hushed voice. "I'm the curious type."

Jake crept along the back wall of the enormous home, bent under a window, and stood up next to the back door. The other two followed close behind. Jake was gently reaching out for the door handle when the door flew open, and he was face-to-face with a startled Kelli. He heard someone yell "No!" and he looked past Kelli to see who was shouting at her. As he did, he saw a man clothed in black tactical gear raise his assault rifle and point it toward Kelli. Jake flung his body on a tangent he hoped would bring him between the shooter and Kelli just as the sharp crack of the weapon echoed through the room.

His attempt to protect Kelli was successful.

A shocked Kelli froze in horror as she watched Jake's body intercept and absorb the killing bullet meant for her. Jake took the bullet in the stomach area and hit the floor with blood already flowing from his abdomen.

Ghost was right behind Jake and saw what was happening. He quickly took out the shooter with a single shot to the head. Matt now exploded through the back door and grabbed Kelli to protect her when he saw Jake's bleeding body on the floor and Ghost kneeling beside him, trying desperately to stem the flow of blood. Ghost knew too well that gut shots were one of the toughest wounds to keep from bleeding out.

Kelli fell to her knees beside a semi-conscious Jake and began sobbing while holding his head in her arms and begging him to hang on.

Ghost ripped open Jake's shirt and tried to get a better look at the wound. He was expertly trained in battlefield triage and first aid.

"How bad is it, Ghost?" Matt asked, half afraid of the answer. He could see it looked bad.

Ghost was still trying to apply pressure, but the wound was bleeding from different sources, and it was impossible to stop it all at the same time with only your hands. He was inwardly cursing the slug from the assault rifle that was designed to penetrate the body and then tumble and move around, causing damage in multiple places before sometimes exiting the body from a different place than where it entered.

"I won't blow smoke up your ass, Matt. This is bad … real bad. He's bleeding out quickly, and I don't think there's any way we can get him to a hospital before that happens. His pulse is already very weak, and his breathing is shallow and erratic."

Matt fell across his old friend's quiet, bloody body, and prayed more fervently than he ever had in his life.

No God, no … not this. Please. Not Jake. He doesn't deserve this. It's all my fault for involving him in this crazy mess. First Lucien, and now Jake? I can't live with this. God, please … please help me. No, I mean help Jake! If you are listening at all … please hear me and don't take Jake away from me …

And the blood continued to flow.

CHAPTER 72

Onboard CIA Choppers
McLean, Virginia

"Put us down … put us down, now!" Agent Milburn barked into his intercom to the pilots of the two choppers approaching the church parking lot where they had chosen to land.

The skilled helicopter pilots pushed it to the danger point and bounced to a landing without actually crashing. The two CIA teams poured out of the choppers and quickly headed to their pre-selected positions near the senator's mansion. First Team stormed quickly up the street that led to the residence and noticed the front gates were wide open, and things did not look right.

"Alright, men, it looks like someone may have arrived before we did. So, we don't know who or what else we may be facing. Second Team, change of plan. Come on up to reinforce First Team. Let's get through that front door now!"

The two teams split to each side of the lane leading to the mansion, ducking in and out of the trees and hedges. They recognized many other boot prints in the damp ground, indicating someone else had taken the same route they were using. They reached the front door without incident and burst through without hesitation, advancing straight to where they heard noises.

There was plenty of surprise to go around from everyone in the house as the CIA teams poured into the sitting room screaming, "FREEZE … CIA!"

The groggy senator and his family and guests were already frozen into position with their hands in the air.

The EDF commandos quickly swung their weaponry in the direction of the CIA teams. The CIA teams responded by leveling their weapons at the EDF teams. Both Agent Milburn and the EDF commander were shouting out orders at the other side to drop their weapons and surrender. There was no indication from either side that this would be happening. It was a tense and deadly standoff with itchy fingers on triggers. Moments as long as days went by with neither side lowering their weapons nor signaling a change in their intent.

Suddenly, the EDF commander moved behind the senator, positioning him between himself and the CIA operatives. He drew his sidearm and pointed it at the senator's temple. He then issued an ultimatum.

"All CIA agents, drop your weapons NOW, or lose a U. S. senator. I don't think that would be an acceptable course of action for CIA agents sworn to allegiance to this country and its corrupt government, do you?"

"We can't do that," Milburn replied. As much as I would not have harm come to Senator Lange, the mission we have been tasked with takes priority even over the life of a senator. I don't know who you guys are, but you are outnumbered and outgunned. So you need to give it up."

"We are outnumbered as far as you can see, but what you can't see is we have additional forces arrayed outside this house, and I think the lady and the relics you are looking for just ran right into their arms. This fight was over before it started, it seems to me," the commander said.

"I have no way of verifying any of that, and I think you're trying to bluff your way out of this. Now give it up and lay down your weapons." Milburn responded.

"I assure you it is not a bluff, Mr. CIA. In fact, I am sure my men have secured the relics and have already made their way off the property. My only mission right now is to see they get as much of a head start as I can provide for them by keeping you and your men engaged right here. So, it looks like we are at an impasse."

"If we have to shoot our way out of here and recover those relics, then so be it," Milburn said through clenched teeth. "Men, prepare to engage and fire on my command!"

"Oh, Mr. CIA, you don't want to do that. I fear things will not go well for the senator here. And we don't want that now, do we? It would be a sad and needless thing to happen considering you have already lost the relics," the commander retorted. "EDF Teams, prepare to defend yourselves. Shoot to kill and for maximum effectiveness. All weapons on full auto, and do not avoid any targets."

Milburn and the commander stared hard at each other for several moments, trying to discern the true intentions of the other and whether either would blink at this last fateful moment.

Neither would.

"Take 'em down!" Milburn shouted.

"Fire!" the commander thundered at the top of his lungs as he began applying pressure to the trigger of the pistol he had against the senator's head.

The senator could barely move his head, but out of the corner of his eye, he could see Hans, Phil, and Lindsay close their eyes.

A blinding flash of brilliant white light instantly filled the room, engulfing everyone in its embrace, and everything … stopped.

The End (for the moment)

To be continued in
Book Three of the Atlantis Legacy Series.

ACKNOWLEDGMENTS

I wish to acknowledge my wife Karole's never-ending support and encouragement of my writing projects. She is always the one that sees my rough drafts, and her feedback is invaluable.

I want to thank my First Readers, Tom Reed and Mel Milburn, for their thoughts and contributions.

Special thanks to Paula Wiseman for her editing skills. My book is leaner and cleaner due to her efforts.

Last but not least…I am eternally grateful to my readers. You are why I write.

Larry Hamilton

Jake is knocking on death's door . . . can he possibly survive?

What is the outcome of the encounter between the CIA and the EDF?

Is it possible for Matt and Kelli to remain free and in possession of the Atlantis Codes? If so . . . what will he decide to do with them?

These questions and many more will be answered in Book Three of the Atlantis Legacy Series . . . The Covenant.

Look for it in the near future at your favorite online booksellers.

I always love to hear from my readers. Please feel free to send me your thoughts at www.HamiltonHouseBooks.com